ELVIS HAS NOT LEFT THE BUILDING

ELVIS HAS NOT LEFT THE BUILDING

A Mystery Novel

J. R. Rain

ACCLAIM FOR THE NOVELS OF J.R. RAIN:

"Be prepared to lose sleep!"
—**James Rollins**, international bestselling author of *Bloodline*

"I love this!"
—**Piers Anthony**, bestselling author of *Xanth*

"J.R. Rain delivers a blend of action and wit that always entertains. Quick with the one-liners, but his characters are fully fleshed out (even the undead ones) and you'll come back again and again."
—**Scott Nicholson**, bestselling author of *The Red Church*

"*Dark Horse* is the best book I've read in a long time!"
—**Gemma Halliday**, award-winning author of *Spying in high Heels*

"*Moon Dance* is absolutely brilliant!"
—**Lisa Tenzin-Dolma**, author of *Understanding the Planetary Myths*

"*Moon Dance* is a must read. If you like Janet Evanovich's Stephanie Plum, bounty hunter, be prepared to love J.R. Rain's Samantha Moon, vampire private investigator."
—**Eve Paludan**, author of *Letters from David*

OTHER BOOKS BY J.R. RAIN

STANDALONE NOVELS
The Lost Ark
Elvis Has *Not* Left the Building
The Body Departed
Silent Echo
Winter Wind

SHORT STORY SINGLES
The Bleeder

VAMPIRE FOR HIRE
Moon Dance
Vampire Moon
American Vampire
Moon Child
Christmas Moon
Vampire Dawn
Vampire Games
Moon Island
Moon River
Vampire Sun
Moon Dragon

SAMANTHA MOON SHORT STORIES
Teeth
Vampire Nights
Vampires Blues
Vampire Dreams
Halloween Moon
Vampire Gold
Blue Moon
Dark Side of the Moon

JIM KNIGHTHORSE SERIES
Dark Horse
The Mummy Case
Hail Mary
Clean Slate
Night Run

JIM KNIGHTHORSE SHORT STORIES
Easy Rider

THE WITCHES TRILOGY
The Witch and the Gentleman
The Witch and the Englishman
The Witch and the Huntsman

THE SPINOZA TRILOGY
The Vampire With the Dragon Tattoo
The Vampire Who Played Dead
The Vampire in the Iron Mask

THE AVALON DUOLOGY
The Grail Quest
The Grail Knight

SHORT STORY COLLECTIONS
The Bleeder and Other Stories
The Santa Call and Other Stories
Vampire Rain and Other Stories

THE VAMPIRE DIARIES
Bound By Blood

SCREENPLAYS
Dark Quests

CO-AUTHORED BOOKS

COLLABORATIONS
Cursed! (with Scott Nicholson)
Ghost College (with Scott Nicholson)
The Vampire Club (with Scott Nicholson)
Dragon Assassin (with Piers Anthony)
Dolfin Tayle (with Piers Anthony)
Jack and the Giants (with Piers Anthony)
Judas Silver (with Elizabeth Basque)
Lost Eden (with Elizabeth Basque)
Deal With the Devil (with Elizabeth Basque)

NICK CAINE ADVENTURES
with Aiden James
Temple of the Jaguar
Treasure of the Deep
Pyramid of the Gods

THE ALADDIN TRILOGY
with Piers Anthony
Aladdin Relighted
Aladdin Sins Bad
Aladdin and the Flying Dutchman

THE WALKING PLAGUE TRILOGY
with Elizabeth Basque
Zombie Patrol
Zombie Rage
Zombie Mountain

THE SPIDER TRILOGY
with Scott Nicholson and H.T. Night
Bad Blood
Spider Web
Spider Bite

THE PSI TRILOGY
with A.K. Alexander
Hear No Evil
See No Evil
Speak No Evil

THE ABNORM CHRONICLES
with Eve Paludan
Glimmer

Elvis Has *Not* Left the Building
Published by J.R. Rain
Copyright © 2010 by J.R. Rain
All rights reserved.
Cover design by Susanna Ivy at:
susannaivy@gmail.com

License Notes
This book is licensed for your personal enjoyment only. This book may not be re-sold. Thank you for respecting the hard work of this author.

ISBN: 1502509148
ISBN 13: 9781502509147

DEDICATION

To my brother, Jason. A true storyteller.

ACKNOWLEDGMENT

A very special thank you to Sandy Johnston for all her help.

THE DREAM

"What's your name?"
"Elvis Presley."
The dream is always the same. I'm in jail. No, I'm in an interrogation room, being questioned for an alleged crime. A murder. My *own* murder.

Somehow, I'm able to see through the one-way mirror. Watching me, hidden behind the glass, aren't just the homicide detectives, but everyone I had ever known, including my ex-wife, my daughter, my mother and even my still-born twin brother, Jessie, now full-grown and looking remarkably like me in my heyday. The media is there, too, of course. Always the media. Every reporter in the land is standing there, watching me, writing fiercely, covering the mother of all tabloid stories.

I feel sick, nauseous. My world is crumbling around me. The accusing detectives smile wickedly and shine a powerful desk lamp directly into my eyes. Cigarette smoke fills the air, hanging there like a roiling gray curtain, filling my nostrils and stinging my eyes. One of the officers blows more of the stuff directly into my face.

"What's your real name?" he asks me.
"Elvis Presley."
"Bullshit." More smoke, more lamps, more light. "What's your full name, goddammit?"
"Elvis Aaron Presley."
"He's dead!" screams the detective.
"No," I say carefully. *"I'm not."*

From behind the one-way mirror, which looks, in fact, more like a window, someone suddenly bursts into tears. It's my daughter, and she buries her face in her mother's shoulder. I'm not supposed to be able to see this display through the one-way mirror, but I can. I always can. Apparently, in my dreams, I have X-ray vision.

I'm still staring at my weeping daughter when a hand turns me violently around, forcing me to look up into a glaring light. I can't see who's silhouetted before me.

"You killed him," says the voice. The voice sounds like it could be my own.

"No, I didn't," I say. "It was a hoax."

"A hoax?" The voice grows enraged. Now it sounds like a multitude of voices, a cacophony erupting from my legions of fans. A universal outlet for all those I had let down, hurt, or disappointed.

"I needed out," I say, babbling, nearly incoherent. "I needed to start over. Everything…everything was so crazy."

I hear more weeping. I turn my head around. It's still my daughter. Always my daughter. Always weeping. And it kills me. She won't look at me, and it breaks my heart more than you know.

"Look at what you've done to her," says the voice, and now I'm sure it's my own voice.

"I'm sorry," I say.

"Say it to *her*."

I look over at my baby, my mouth open to speak, but no words come out. Someone smacks me hard across the face, rocking me. I nearly topple out of the chair. My hands, I realize, are tied behind me, as if I had been kidnapped.

"Who are you?" screams the voice.

"Elvis—"

"Bullshit."

"Who are you?"

"I don't know. Not anymore…."

"Who are you?"

And here is when I always wake up, tears streaming down my cheeks, always alone in my tiny single apartment in Los Angeles, just down the road from the various studios where I had made so many of my early films. My blankets are often on the floor and I'm usually covered in sweat. My head often pounds from the usual hangover. I usually never go back to sleep. I don't want to dream the dream again. I don't want to see my daughter's pain.

* * *

This morning was no different.

I awoke with a start, bolting upright, momentarily disoriented. My blankets were on the floor again, as if I had been fighting a monster in my sleep. I could still hear the accusing voice in my head, but this time it belonged to my twin brother—my *dead* twin brother who had died at birth. I heard his voice now, clearly, eerily, reaching up through the depths of my subconscious and down through the ages, spoken in a voice that sounded remarkably like my own.

"Today is our birthday, Elvis. But, of course, since I was born dead, today is also my *deathday*. Ironic isn't it?"

Yes, I thought, *ironic*.

I sat back in bed, closed my eyes, ran my fingers through my thick hair. Tomorrow I see my shrink.

Thank God.

CHAPTER ONE

This is going to hurt.

My apartment was empty. I was standing in my bathroom, dressed in boxers and nothing else. I was about to look very foolish and I was glad there was no one else here to witness it.

Hell, I was almost embarrassed for myself.

With one of my own songs playing in the background, I slowly started gyrating my hips. Just a little. Nothing too wild. Nothing like I used to do. And already I could feel a tingle of pain going up my back.

Yeah, this is going to hurt.

But I wanted to do it. I *had to do* it. For quite some time now I had felt the itch.

And it was a hell of an itch.

I picked up the pace a little. I felt clumsy and out of sync. I stumbled once or twice as my bare feet slapped against the cold linoleum floor. One of my swaying hips nailed the bathroom door knob, sending the door itself slamming back into the bathroom wall. I think the drywall might have cracked.

But I continued doing my thing. My crazy thing.

Mercifully, the clumsiness quickly faded. Amazingly, wonderfully, flashes of my old self came back. I quickly worked up a sweat. My belly, round and full, pulled on my lower back. The strain was nearly unbearable.

God, I needed to lose weight. So easy to let yourself go when you don't care.

But, lately, I had started caring. And slowly but surely I had started changing my diet. A salad here. A banana there. Venti mochas reluctantly switched to grande mochas.

I tried another move. A patented move. One that had driven the women of the world crazy—

I swung my leg and hip out, and screamed in pain. I lurched over the bathroom sink, gasping. Something pulled. I hunched there over the bathroom sink, gasping, sweating, staring at myself in the mirror. Gray hair. Custom-built face. Wrinkles.

God, the wrinkles….

It's hell getting old.

A loud knock on my front door. I sucked in some air, willed myself to stand upright. On knees that were already stiffening, I made my way to the front door, limping slightly, knuckling my lower back.

I checked the peephole. It was my eighty-year-old downstairs neighbor, Mrs. Haynesworth. I opened the door.

"Sorry for the noise, Mrs. Haynesworth."

"Well, my granddaughter's asleep. And all that banging up here." She squinted at me, peering through her remarkably thick glasses. Sometimes I thought she knew my super-secret identity. Then again, with her eyesight, I always shrugged off the feeling. "What are you doing up here, anyway?"

"Trying out my dance moves."

"Dance moves? Mr. King, you're far too old to be dancing. You might hurt yourself."

I smiled. "I'll keep the noise down, Mrs. Haynesworth. Have a good day."

She continued peering at me as I closed the door. I hobbled into the kitchen—and popped a Vicodin or two.

Or three.

CHAPTER TWO

The doorbell rang.

I was sitting in a comfortable loveseat I had scavenged for free from Craigslist.com, watching a TV that I had recently found on the side of the road, surrounded by tables and lamps and artwork that I had purchased for cheap from local garage sales.

Oh, how the mighty have fallen.

It was the middle of a bright winter day and I was watching Oprah, of course. What else was there to do? I liked Oprah. I think she and I would have gotten along just fine. Anyway, she was having a special tribute to the King, being that it was his birthday.

That it was *my* birthday.

Sitting beside her were two women: Elvis Presley's ex-wife and his daughter. Both looking radiant. Both looking breath-takingly beautiful, especially his daughter. *My daughter.* Of course, my daughter also looked sad and lost and heartbroken. Always sad. Always lost. Always heart broken.

Damn.

The doorbell rang again.

I ignored it and, entranced, continued watching Oprah's special tribute to the King, and when the show was finally over, when I had seen enough commercials for feminine hygiene products to last a life time, I was a total emotional wreck. Hell, the collar to my polo shirt was even wet with my tears. Oddly, my knuckles hurt as well—and not just from my arthritis. Apparently, while watching the show, I had been clawing the hell out of the armrest of my recently acquired love seat.

In fact, I had torn the seam of it a little. Damn. Then again, perhaps it was already torn? Hard to tell with free furniture.

Oprah waved goodbye to the camera, and as she did so I watched my daughter look away and bite her lower lip, seemingly stifling a sob.

Damn.

As the show went to commercial, I heaved myself up from the sunken love seat, somehow straining my right knee in the process. The roadside TV didn't come with a remote, so I manually clicked the thing off the old fashioned way. As I did so, high on a bookshelf next to the TV, I found myself staring at a picture of the very same girl who had just been sitting next to Oprah. Except the girl in the picture was a little girl and she was sitting high on her tiny pony, smiling the world's biggest smile. *A girl and her pony, it's a beautiful thing.* She had loved that pony and she had loved me. She looked so happy back then, so alive and happy.

So how could I break her heart?

Therein lies the rub.

She hasn't looked happy in some time. Trust me, I know this. I study every picture I can get my hands on, minutely, agonizing over the details. Was she healthy? (Yes, from all indications.) Was she happy? (No, not for a long time, but I've been wrong before.) And today she had looked utterly and completely miserable. The sadness in her distant, round eyes ran as deep as wells.

Outside, someone started a lawnmower. I sighed and stepped over to the living room window. Outside, a small Hispanic man was pushing a lawnmower across a swath of grass that ran in front of my apartment complex. Sweat streamed down his caramel-colored skin. The lawnmower was almost as big as he was.

Up the street, double-parked, was a UPS truck. A bum was currently urinating on its right rear tire. The bum had just managed to stumble away before a fit young man with hairy legs trotted out of a nearby apartment complex and hopped up into the truck and sped away.

And that's when I remembered the doorbell.

Ah, yes, all that damn ringing.

I moved away from the window, past Kendra the Wonder Kat, who currently lay sleeping in a furry striped ball in the center of my reading chair—no doubt dreaming of mice and toys and things that go squeak in the night—and opened my front door.

Bright sunshine poured in. Painfully bright sunshine. I shielded my eyes, blinking hard, and there, sitting on the little-used welcome mat, was a thick envelope.

The package was addressed to *E.P.*

CHAPTER THREE

I sat at my kitchen table with the package. The small hairs at the back of my neck were standing on end, as if a goose had walked across my grave.

Or perhaps across my *brother's* grave.

Despite myself, I looked over my shoulder, peering down the short hallway to my bedroom. I was alone, of course. Still, I had a sense that I was being watched, and I *hate* that sense.

I turned back to the package, a package that was addressed to one E.P.

Hands shaking, heart hammering, I tore through the padded envelope with a thick and slightly broken fingernail, and removed a clear plastic box containing a watch. On the face of it was Elvis Presley dancing, doing that crazy thing he does with his legs. The watch even showed the correct time. Inside the padded envelope was also a tightly folded piece of paper. I took it out and, with increasingly unsteady fingers, unfolded it.

It was hotel stationery from the Embassy Suites here in Los Angeles. Just two words were written across the middle of it in small, neat cursive: *Happy Birthday.*

I stared at the letter for some time, my mind running through a possible list of stalking candidates, and came up with nothing. Finally, I opened the plastic case and put the watch on—and kinda liked it. It would go well with my already sizable collection of Elvis memorabilia. I'm a nerd like that.

My cover was blown, that much was for sure. By whom I did not know, and how long before *Access Hollywood* came knocking at my door, I didn't know, either.

Numb and sick to my stomach, I pushed away from the table and went over and sat at my desk in the far corner of the living room. I found a plain manila case folder and wrote "Stalker" on the tab. There, now it was official. I had me a stalker. I slipped the note inside, along with the padded envelope, and filed the whole thing away in my dilapidated filing cabinet that I had gotten for free from a retired doctor.

In my bathroom, from the medicine cabinet, I found my little bottle of pick-me-up pills. Vicodin. My preferred drug of the day. I tapped out three fat pills, poured myself a cup of sink water and knocked them back one at a time like a whooping crane downing sardines.

In the kitchen, from a cupboard above the sink, I found my not-so-hidden bottle of Jack Daniels. I unscrewed the cap and drank it straight, and I kept on drinking until I finally felt better.

CHAPTER FOUR

We were at a Starbucks in Silver Lake, which is a hilly district east of Hollywood. Yes, there was even a lake here. Granted, it was a reservoir surrounded by an eight-foot high chain-linked fence topped with barbed wire, but, hey, that's L.A. for you.

I was eating a $1.60 old-fashioned chocolate donut that tasted remarkably like a .60 cent old-fashioned chocolate donut. Across from me, drinking a mocha something-or-other, was an old friend. A very *trusted* old friend. Clarke McGuire was a defense attorney here in L.A. Five years ago, Clarke hired me to help clear one of his clients of murder. The case started simple, but ended bad. Very bad. Someone had ended up dead, and Clarke and I had been at the wrong place at the wrong time, and suddenly we had a body to dump. And so we did, together, in the desert, in a grave we dug together. Call it a bonding experience. Now we shared a secret that we would take to our own graves, and since we were sharing secrets, I had let him in on a big one of my own.

Now Clarke McGuire, defense attorney, with his perfectly bald head and too big hands, was one of only three people on Earth who knew that Elvis Presley was living in obscurity in L.A. and working secretly as a private investigator.

Unless you counted the stalker.

Without looking up from his newspaper, Clarke said, "Happy birthday, by the way."

"Is that why you splurged for the donut?" I asked.

"That, and because you're broke again."

"Well, you're a day late," I said. "My birthday was yesterday."

"I'm a day late, and you're a dollar short."

"Oh, brother," I said.

Clarke chuckled to himself, turned the page, snapped the paper taut.

Starbucks was filled nearly to capacity. We sat alone in a corner, near the front entrance, at the only rectangular table the place offered, a table which was designated for the handicapped. I knew this because a little yellow wheelchair was routed into the wooden surface. I wasn't handicapped, and neither was Clarke. By all rights, this was an illegal coffee affair.

"We're sitting at the handicap table," I said.

"I know."

"Neither of us is handicapped," I said, "unless we count your baldness."

"Baldness isn't a handicap."

"Should be."

He shook his head. His *bald* head, that is. "I tried calling you yesterday," he said. "Your phone was off. Wanted to wish you a happy birthday."

"I hate my birthday."

"I know."

I was quiet. Clarke was reading the *L.A. Times*, or at least pretending to. More often than not, I caught him watching me. Clarke was a good friend, my only friend, but he was also infatuated with me. Sometimes I wished I had never divulged my secret to him. Surprise, it turned out he was quite the Elvis fan. Lucky me.

"She was on TV yesterday," I said. "Oprah."

Clarke nodded; he knew who *she* was. "How'd she look?"

"Beautiful," I said. "And sad. Always sad."

I was tracing the engraving of the wheelchair with my finger, listening to the chatter of orders at the nearby counter, everyone speaking a secret Starbucks language, meaningless to the uninitiated. I was suddenly wishing my drink had something stronger in it than just a shot or two of espresso.

"I'd do anything to see her again, Clarke."

"I know."

"Just one minute. One hug."

"Dead men don't give hugs."

"Thank you, Davy Jones."

He chuckled and turned back to his paper. We were silent some more. Starbucks was alive and well and running on caffeine. A few minutes later, without looking up, Clarke said, "I have a job for you if you're interested. Missing person case."

Working was good for me. It kept me sane. Kept my thoughts in check, my mind in check. It was damn easy for my life to spiral out of control if I let it. Working hard and helping others kept me grounded, alive. It also put food on my table.

"Tell me about it," I said.

"Missing female. Twenty-two, an actress. Missing now for three days."

"Haven't heard about it."

"And you won't. The mother wants to keep this quiet, if possible. Her daughter has a movie coming out this fall, and the mother doesn't want the bad publicity."

"Nice to see her priorities are in order."

Clarke shrugged. "Not my business," he said. "Ideally the girl is found safe and sound and the public is none the wiser."

"Except the public might have leads to her whereabouts."

"What can I say," he said. "I'm just their attorney."

"Fine," I said, "What does the LAPD have so far?"

"So far nothing, which is why the mother is hiring every available PI she can find."

"Even old ones?" I asked.

"Even old ones," said Clarke. "I told her that you're the best in the business at finding the missing, that, in fact, it's your specialty."

I finished the last of the donut. "Sometimes they're found dead, Clarke," I said.

"I know," he said. "I left that part out."

CHAPTER FIVE

She was an Elvis Presley fan and she was dying. I knew this because the *L.A. Times* did a write up on her in the Community section of the paper. I had been flipping through the paper after Clarke left Starbucks. It's hard to miss a color photo of a little girl with an Elvis wig and sideburns and dressed in rhinestones and wearing my aviator glasses. Well, hard to miss for me, at least. I stopped turning the pages and read the article. She was in the final stages of leukemia, and her prognosis was not good. Although not stated directly, the impression I got from the article was that she should have been dead months ago. Miraculously, she hung on, and on the days when she was feeling better, she would entertain the other kids with her Elvis impersonation. Apparently, she was pretty good. Most striking was that she was a foster child, having spent her life predominately in the California foster program, having never found a home. She was only seven and my heart broke for her.

Which was why, an hour or two later, I found myself in the Good Samaritan Hospital in Los Angeles, making my way down an empty, carpeted corridor with flowers in hand. *Flowers and a special gift*. I was in the pediatrics oncology wing, where they treated children with cancer.

I approached the nurse's desk, manned by two nurses. One of them looked up at me and smiled.

"How can I help you?"

"I'm here to see Beth Ann Morgan."

She smiled warmly. "Ah, our little Elvis. She's been getting a lot of attention with that article. Lots of flowers and cards." She pointed to a nearby room. The door was open and from within I could see an abundance of flowers and bobbing helium balloons. "But no one has come to see her personally."

I nodded, unsure of what to say, and so I spoke from my heart. "I was touched by her story."

The nurse studied me, nodding. "We all are. She's very special to us." She studied me some more. "Obviously you are not family."

Left unsaid was that I was obviously not family since Beth Ann Morgan had no family. I shook my head. "No, ma'am, but I would really like to see her."

She continued looking at me. "She's very sick. She's taken a turn for the worse."

"I'm sorry to hear that, but I would still like to see her."

Now we had gotten the attention of the other nurse, and both of them were looking at me. The second nurse said, "Well, see if she wants any visitors. It couldn't hurt."

The first nurse nodded and stood. "Okay, but one of us will be with you at all times."

"I understand."

"Who should I say you are?"

"Just tell her I'm a fellow Elvis fan."

She grinned. "Aren't we all."

She disappeared into the nearby room, and a moment later she came back. "Okay, Beth Ann will see you."

CHAPTER SIX

The figure on the bed was tiny, wasting away.

Beth Ann was still wearing her Elvis wig and sideburns, although the left sideburn currently sat askew on her face. She was wearing a rhinestone jacket. It was something cheap, probably from a Halloween shop. Her plastic Elvis aviator glasses were sitting on the swing-out table next to her. As I stepped into the room, I found her sitting up in bed, although I sensed she had recently been asleep. Still, she smiled brightly at me, and there was no indication in her smile—or in her sweet face—that she was very near death.

The nurse sat in a chair behind me and allowed me to approach the little girl, and I did so, stopping at the foot of her bed. Her feet projected up through the thin fabric of the hospital comforter about halfway down the bed. She was a tiny little girl; no doubt getting tinier each day, wasting away.

"Hi," I said.

"Hi," she said.

"What's your name?" I asked.

"Beth Ann."

"That's a pretty name. My name's Aaron."

Her eyes widened briefly. Lord, she looked ridiculous in her Elvis wig and sideburns. Ridiculous and damned cute. I wanted to hug her. I also realized that she was, no doubt, bald beneath her wig.

"Elvis's middle name was Aaron," she said.

"Oh, really?" I said. "You know a lot about Elvis, huh?"

"I know *everything* about Elvis! I love him!"

"Do you know when he was born?" I asked.

"January eighth, nineteen thirty-five."

"And when he died?"

"August sixteenth, nineteen seventy-seven."

"Wow, you do know a lot about Elvis."

"I told you."

"Yup, you sure did. I believe you now."

"I'm an expert."

"I can see that," I said. "So why do you like Elvis so much?"

Her face lit up. "He's so cute."

"Cute?" I said. "You're too young to think he's cute."

"No. He's cute no matter how old you are."

It was hard for me to argue with that logic. "What else do you like about Elvis?"

"He was the best singer *ever*. But I don't just like him. I *love* him."

"Excuse me. I stand corrected."

"But I also love him because he is my friend."

"Your friend?" I said.

"I mean, I know he's not my *real* friend, but sometimes when I look at his pictures or watch his movies, or listen to his music, I think he is talking to me, or singing to me, or looking at me, and he makes me so happy because I don't feel so alone."

I almost lost it right there. Tears sprung to eyes, but somehow I kept it together. I said, "I'm sorry you feel so alone, sweetheart."

"It's okay. I'm used to it."

I looked over at the nurse sitting behind us. The woman, obviously exhausted, had her eyes closed and seemed to be dozing, but I doubted it. She was sneaking in a break, true, but I suspected she was also listening to every word, as well.

"So what's your last name, Aaron?" the little girl asked, sitting up some more.

"King," I said.

"Serious?"

"Serious," I said.

"But Elvis was known as the King."

"Perhaps it's just a lucky coincidence," I said.

She studied me, pursing her lips slightly. "How old are you?" she asked.

"Seventy-four."

She started counting rapidly on her fingers, and when she was finished, she looked completely confused. "Elvis would have been seventy-four, too."

"Wow, now that is a coincidence, isn't it?"

"What does *coincidence* mean? You keep saying it."

"It means that life can be very interesting sometimes."

She shrugged, but seemed to like my answer, and smiled brightly. Her smile broke my heart because, really, she had nothing to smile about. Nothing but Elvis.

"I brought you some flowers," I said.

"I like flowers!"

I noted that she only *liked* flowers, but she *loved* Elvis. I held out the flat box. "I also got you this."

"What is it?"

"You'll have to open it and see." The moment the words came out of my mouth I realized my mistake. She didn't have the strength to open the box, much less hold onto it. "But maybe I can open it for you," I added.

"Sure!"

And so I did, setting the box down on the foot of her hospital bed and untying the red ribbon. As I pulled the lid off the box, Beth Ann sat forward in bed, trying to peer into the box. I next lifted out one of my original rhinestone jackets I had worn back in the early seventies. Beth Ann's jaw dropped, and it kept on dropping.

"It's Elvis's jacket," she said.

"Yes," I said.

"Is it real?"

"Very real."

"Oh my gosh, oh my gosh, oh my gosh!"

"Would you like to try it on?"

"Are you serious?"

"Well, it's yours now. You can do whatever you want with it."

"I want to wear it!"

"I'm sorry, she can't," said the nurse behind us. "She's hooked up to an IV."

But with a little pleading on my part, and a lot of begging on Beth Anne's part, the nurse gave in, and a few minutes later, after some careful maneuvering, the jacket was on the little girl and the IV was back in place. Except the jacket looked more like a glittering robe on her, but I don't think she cared much. She snuggled deeply in it, and ran her little hands over it for quite a while, all while making tiny, imperceptible little noises.

"That was awfully nice of you," said the nurse.

"It's the least I could do."

She patted me on the shoulder and slipped around me and sat back in her chair. She closed her eyes and said, "Trust me, you could have done far less."

I smiled, but she didn't see me smile. I looked back to Beth Ann, who was still caressing the sleeves.

"Elvis really wore this?" she asked, her little noises finally forming into words.

"Yes," I said.

"You swear?"

"I swear. It was, in fact, his favorite."

"But how do you know—?"

Beth Ann never finished her sentence. In fact, her words seemed to have gotten stuck somewhere in her throat. She looked up at me so sharply that her Elvis wig flopped over to one side. She ignored the wig and studied me carefully, and, for the second time in a matter of minutes, her mouth dropped open. This time it stayed open. It took the innocence of a child to see through me.

"Elvis?" she said.

I looked back at the nurse, but the nurse appeared to be asleep. I turned to Beth Ann and raised my finger to my lips. "Our secret, okay?"

She nodded, or tried to. Her eyes had somehow grown another inch or two in diameter. I don't think she had blinked in a long, long time.

"Would you like for me to sing to you?" I asked.

She nodded again, and now tears filled her eyes and spilled out. I picked up a nearby plastic chair, brought it over to the side of her bed, and sat next to her. I gently took her tiny hand in mine and cleared my throat. And then I sang to her quietly, my voice low and meant only for her. As I sang, my old voice broke often, especially when I looked into this little girl's eyes, this forgotten girl with no family or home, no parents or brothers or sisters. A sweet little angel who spent her own time cheering up other sick kids by dressing up as Elvis and singing to them. I squeezed her hand gently as I sang songs I hadn't sung in thirty years. Sometimes Beth Ann sang with me, and hers was the sweetest voice I had ever heard in my life. But then she would grow weak and stop and just watch me with her impossibly huge eyes and hold my hands and cry softly.

And when the nurse finally touched my shoulder and told me that Beth Ann needed to rest, I leaned down and kissed the little girl on her forehead.

"Will you be back?" she asked.

"Every day," I said.

Except she didn't have another day. The next morning when I returned bearing more gifts—a pair of my original aviator glasses and a signed album cover—the same nurse who had sat with us looked up from the pediatric desk, shook her head sadly, and told me Beth Ann had passed in the night.

I heard later she had been buried in my jacket, and that most of the hospital staff had been there at her funeral.

Rest in peace, little darlin'.

And now, every Saturday evening, an old man who sounded remarkably like Elvis Presley, sang songs to the children at Good Samaritan Hospital in Los Angeles, carrying on Beth Ann's tradition.

It was the least I could do.

CHAPTER SEVEN

Kelly was my on-again/off-again girlfriend. Mostly we were *off-again*, as we had some serious issues. Mostly they were trust issues. As in, she didn't trust me. As in, she felt I was holding something back. Ya think? Presently, we were *on-again*.

"I have a confession," she said.

Don't we all, I thought.

I waited. We were in a small restaurant here in Echo Park, a one-time cop-shop called The Brite Spot—and it was a rather bright spot on a fairly bleak stretch of Sunset Blvd. We were sitting across from each other in an old-school booth with deeply padded vinyl cushions. Kelly, normally calm and confident, was looking increasingly nervous and agitated. She was drinking some freshly squeezed orange juice and couldn't decide whether to hold it or set it down. I was having decaf coffee, which I didn't have any problem holding. As I sipped, the steam from my coffee obscured Kelly's face into a sort of wavering, haunting mirage of a one-time beautiful actress who had taken the non-enhancement high road and let herself age gracefully. Now, too old to find steady work, she worked behind the scenes managing young talent. Well respected in the industry, I knew her to be fair and honest, a true bright spot of her own in this sometimes seedy business.

"I've hired a private investigator," she said suddenly, blurting out the words.

I said nothing, although my heart rate immediately doubled the moment her words registered. I waited, viewing her from over the coffee mug, using it to hide my face. The Brite Spot didn't serve alcohol for reasons unknown. I hate that.

Kelly took a swig of her orange juice, knocking it back. Very unladylike. I continued saying nothing. Continued hiding behind my mug until I could get control of my emotions.

"Yes, a private investigator," she said again, averting her eyes from mine. "I know how secretive you are and I knew this would upset you, but I don't care anymore, Aaron. For us to move forward—for our relationship to really move forward—I need some answers, and I'm not getting them from you."

I finally set down my steaming mug. A private investigator was digging into my past, perhaps even at this very moment. A past that needed to stay hidden. A past that needed to stay dead to the world. Blood pounded in my ears.

Kelly, unfortunately, was a one-woman gossip mill, unable to keep even the smallest of secrets to herself. Hell, half the rumors in Hollywood were spread because of her. It was because of this that I could never fully trust her with my own secret. One of the reasons why we were mostly an off-again couple.

When I disappeared from the world, I knew dating and having a girlfriend would be risky. Secrets were spilled, and mistakes were made. Which was why I mostly hadn't dated, and why I lived alone. You can't divulge secrets when you're alone.

Of course, all that went out the window the day I met Kelly. It wasn't love at first site, granted, but the chemistry was right and the connection was real. But my inability to trust her with my innermost secret continued to sabotage our relationship. She knew I was holding back, and it was driving her crazy.

It was a quagmire, sure, but I did my best to navigate through it. And if it meant fibbing to her on occasion, well, that was just too bad. Too much was at stake.

"I see I've upset you," she said. Her fingers were moving rapidly, touching everything within reach. Currently, she was molesting a fork.

I reached out and took her wrists gently, calming her. Now was not a time to show anger—or even panic—over what she had done. I had to diffuse the situation *now*. True, I had taken great pains to conceal my past, even from the most aggressive of private investigators; still, anyone could get lucky and stumble on something I had missed.

As an investigator myself, I knew that as a fact.

I said, "I should have been more up front with you, yes. But I'm very private by nature. I don't mean to be. I'm sorry."

"Jesus, Aaron, we've been dating for nearly three years and I feel I barely know you."

"I'm sorry you feel that way," I said. "I'll work on it."

"Then work on it now, dammit."

"What would you like for me to do?"

"Tell me something I don't know, Aaron. Hell, tell me anything."

"Anything," I said, thinking hard. I had a very detailed script that I used as an old standby. I recalled it now.

In that moment, two cops came in and sat in the booth behind Kelly, wearing the tighter uniforms of biker cops. Or, as I like to think of them, the cool cops.

"Where were you born?" she asked.

"California." A lie.

She frowned, picked up a spoon. Set it down again. Twisted her napkin. Untwisted it.

"Yes, you've told me that. Aaron, my investigator tells me he can't find any birth records in California. Or anywhere, for that matter. Can we talk about that?"

I had to give her something now or she would keep pushing, and keep pushing, and her investigator would keep investigating, and this could all blow up in my face.

Luckily, I had a little something prepared.

"I grew up poor, Kelly. I'm not proud of that; in fact, it's damn embarrassing. I was schooled at home. I never went to high school or college. My father died when I was young and my mother was too sick to work." I took a deep, shuddering my breath. "I dropped out of school at age thirteen and have been working ever since. Look, it's a time of my life that I would just as soon forget."

Hell of a performance, if I do say so myself. My voice had even cracked a little. Who said I couldn't act?

Kelly opened her mouth to speak, but nothing came out. The napkin in her hands had been twisted into shreds.

"But why no birth certificate? Why no military records, no real estate records, or marriage records, or even credit history earlier than a few decades ago. There's nothing."

I looked at her for some time. She held my gaze defiantly. In the past, I would have changed the subject. She knew that. But she was pushing this, and unless I gave her something to chew on, something that would really hold up, this woman could potentially cause my whole house of cards to come tumbling down.

"Kelly, I've done some bad things in my past. I was in trouble. I would have gone to jail…unless I gave up some names."

I kept my voice low and even. No one heard, no one cared, and no one knew what the hell we were talking about. The cops were talking quietly among themselves while keeping a casual eye on those around them. Kelly caught on to me immediately.

"So you gave up the names," she said, conspiratorially. She was loving this, perhaps too much.

"Yes."

"And now you're in the witness protection program."

"Could you say that a little louder?"

"Sorry."

The waiter came by, a very metrosexual-looking kid with rectangular glasses and mussed hair. He topped off my decaf, asked Kelly if she wanted more OJ. She shook her head sharply once; he got the hint and split.

She said, "Can I ask what you did that was so bad?"

"No, not yet," I said, mostly because I didn't know yet myself. "Let's pace this a little, okay?"

"Okay," she said, but I could see that she was humming with excitement, bursting with a need to spread this news. I felt bad for lying, but the bigger picture was far more important.

"This has to be our secret, okay?" I said.

She nodded slowly. Almost reluctantly. "It will be, I promise."

"If you can keep this one secret, perhaps I will tell you more. But you have to prove to me that you can keep this one."

"You sound like you're lecturing a little girl."

"Well, you are fifteen years my junior."

"Okay, fine," she said, sticking out her bottom lip. "I can keep a secret."

"You need to call your investigator off, too."

"Okay, I will," she said.

We were silent. Three loud young men came into the restaurant, spotted the cops and quieted down immediately. Kelly reached out and took both my hands. Her palms were moist.

"I'm sorry, Aaron. I really am. I know this isn't easy for you."

I couldn't let her off the hook. I needed this issue to go away, and I needed to show her how much I was bothered by this. Perhaps then, in the future, she would think twice about pulling another stunt like this.

"No, it's not easy," I said. "Not to mention your private eye might very well jeopardize my life. Kelly, who I was in the past is dead. You have to let that go."

She nodded slowly, and then more vigorously. "I understand, and I'm sorry. I'll call him off tonight." She kept holding my hands, running her thumbs over my thick fingers. "Maybe with this out in the open we can finally move forward. Do you want that?"

I looked up at this beautiful woman who had put up with me for the last few years. Sure, we had our ups and downs. Sure, the *downs* were mostly because of me and my secrets. But she had persevered. She loved me and did not want me for my wealth or fame or because I was the King. She wanted me for *me*, because I made her feel good. And that made me feel damn good, too.

"Yes," I said, squeezing her hand. "I want that."

CHAPTER EIGHT

Dr. Vivian Carter was a small woman with big glasses. She was also my therapist, and as I stepped into her office and eased down into her wingback chair for my weekly appointment, I could feel the weight of her considerable stare upon me now; a weight, no doubt, made more considerable due to her incredibly thick glasses.

A month ago, in one long rambling session, I disclosed to Dr. Vivian my super-secret Elvis identity. I never intended to, but I found myself trusting her deeply, and since all my other problems were tied to this one big issue—this one epic issue—then I was going to have to come clean.

And so I did.

Now, of course, the good Dr. Vivian thought I was a nutcase. And why shouldn't she? Just another loony claiming to be Elvis. Still, *this* loony had given her evidence—*proof*—that I was, in fact, Elvis Presley. Whether or not she chose to believe the evidence was another matter.

Now we were in her office, located on the ground floor of her stately two-story bungalow-style home here in Echo Park. Dr. Vivian sat behind an executive desk that seemed entirely too massive for her small office. Had she been a male therapist, I would have suspected penis compensation issues. Being a female therapist, as it were, I was out of theories. The blinds behind her desk were partly open and the sun was pouring in. As I looked out the window, the small shadow of a small bird flitted by and alighted on a nearby skeletal tree branch. The bird twittered pleasantly. Seconds later, the silhouette of a cat appeared on the window's ledge, creeping toward the bird.

Ah, the wheels of life keep on turning....

Dr. Vivian was forty-seven, petite, and quite the looker; that is, if you liked the nerdy type. And with her it was easy to like the nerdy type. Luckily, no pocket protector.

Admittedly, I had the hots for her. In a bad way, actually. Officially, she was a family and marriage counselor. Unofficially, she took a sort of holistic approach to people and their problems, which is what appealed to me in the first place. After all, I didn't want to know *why* I was messed up. I wanted to know the *greater purpose* behind why I was messed up.

"What would you like to talk about today?" Dr. Vivian asked, completely unaware of the cat stalking the bird directly behind her. And, no doubt, completely unaware that I had it bad for her.

"Let's talk about me for a change," I said.

She smiled but said nothing. Dr. Vivian didn't find me nearly as entertaining as I found myself.

"Actually," I said. "I would like to talk about who I really am."

"Who you really are?" she said, and I could hear the slight disapproval in her voice.

"Unfortunately, doctor, I still think I'm Elvis."

She shifted in her chair and tapped the eraser end of her pencil against a poster-sized desk calendar spread over the surface of her voluminous desk. Numerous scribblings covered the desk calendar. Unfortunately, I was sitting too far away to read the scribblings, although I was admittedly curious. What did therapists scribble about, anyway?

"Fine, let's talk about it. So what is it, exactly, that you want from me, Mr. King?"

"I want you to believe me."

"To believe that you are Elvis Presley?"

"Yes."

"Last week I had a patient tell me he was God."

"Did he turn your Liquid Paper into wine?"

Again, she didn't smile.

"You see my point," she said.

"Yes. You deal with a lot of crazies."

"We don't use the term 'crazy' here. Delusional, perhaps."

"You think I'm delusional?"

"My beliefs are not the issue here."

"I beg to differ," I said. "I need a therapist who believes me, who believes *in* me. A therapist who does not patronize me."

"You're asking a lot of me," she said.

"I think you're up to the challenge."

She studied me. "The easy diagnosis is that you suffer from a dissociative identity disorder."

"In English."

"You think you're someone else."

"Maybe I should have picked Brad Pitt, then."

"This isn't funny, Mr. King."

"Of course not," I said. "So what's your diagnosis?"

She took in some air, held it, tapped her pencil on the calendar some more, then looked me squarely in the eye. "You don't have a dissociative identity disorder."

"I don't?"

"No, Mr. Presley, you don't."

* * *

I stopped breathing. Had I heard her right?

A hint of a smile touched her lips, then spread to her entire face. As it did, a fabulous weight fell from my shoulders and I nearly wept.

"You gave me proof the last time we met," she said. "I checked your proof. Everything checked out." She suddenly stood, leaned across her desk and held out her hand. "Nice to meet you, Mr. Elvis Presley. I'm Dr. Vivian Carter."

Too stunned to speak, I reached numbly across her desk and took her hand.

CHAPTER NINE

"You believe me then?" I asked.

She didn't immediately answer, nor did she release my hand. Instead, she stood there looking down at me, her eyes searching every square inch of my face. Beyond Dr. Vivian, framed nearly perfectly in the window, was the silhouette of the tomcat sitting motionless on the window ledge. The bird, clueless, went about its business energetically, hopping contentedly from branch to branch. Finally, the good doctor released my hand and sat back in her chair.

"I do, Mr. King, but this is highly irregular."

"Highly," I said.

"You have a lot of issues."

"More than you know," I said.

The lens of her considerable glasses caught some of the afternoon sun, nearly blinding me. From behind her desk, she carefully crossed one leg over the other, and from where I sat, I could see some of her exposed knee. Hubba hubba.

"So what made you finally believe me?" I asked.

"The list of names you provided. The plastic surgeon, in particular."

"You called him."

"I did."

"What did he say?"

"Nothing at first. Until I gave him the password. Cute."

"Well, we all have a little hound dog in us, doctor," I said. *Hound dog*, was, of course, the password. Dr. Castro, my plastic surgeon so many years ago and a wonderful friend, had been sworn to silence. Unless he was given the password. "So what did Dr. Castro tell you?"

"He described the surgery he performed on you. Radical face-altering surgery. Nose job, chin implant, reshaping of the ears, mouth, eyes." She paused, studied me again. "He did a wonderful job, you know. You look nothing like him—or you. You know what I mean." Her face actually reddened.

"Yes," I said, smiling. "I know what you mean."

"But now I can see the similarities."

"Lucky me."

The clock on the wall behind me ticked loudly, filling the big room with its small noise. The bird hopped over to another branch, then to another, moving ever closer to the statuesque cat.

Dr. Vivian said, "Admittedly, I was slow to move forward, slow to believe. I mean, you have to understand my hesitation."

"I understand."

"But everything checked out. Everything. Especially the surgeon."

I smiled. "And here you thought I was crazy."

She smiled back at. "The verdict is still out, Mr. King. You did, after all, fake your own death."

"You should try it sometime; it's very liberating."

She ignored that. "We're going to have to start over with your sessions, you know."

"I understand."

"Everything has changed. I mean, you went from being Aaron King to *Elvis fucking Presley*."

"Such language for a therapist."

"I think our once traditional doctor/patient relationship might have flown out the window."

Much like the bird. It suddenly darted off the branch, swooped down, then disappeared from view. The tom watched it go, flattening his ears, his wound-up energy dissipating in an instant. He flicked his tail once, then slinked off.

Dr. Vivian was studying me, completely unaware of the drama behind her. "You have issues with guilt," she said. "And now I see why. You abandoned your daughter."

"You get right to it," I said, shifting.

"You're paying me to help you, not gush over you."

"How much to gush over me?"

She ignored that. "You take painkillers to deal with your guilt."

"You're good," I said.

"You want to stop the pain."

"Yes," I said. "Very much so."

"Life is pain, Mr. King," she said.

"I'm not sure I wanted to hear that."

"Life wasn't meant to be easy. At least, not at first."

"Not at first?"

"Life is about living, and making mistakes. But more importantly, life is about learning from mistakes. With growth, mistakes are not repeated, and thus the path becomes smoother. You are stuck in a cycle of repeating your same mistakes."

"So what do I do?" I asked.

"It's time to learn from your mistakes, Aaron. It's time to grow up."

"I'm too old to grow up," I said.

She smiled and might have gushed a little. "You're never too old."

CHAPTER TEN

Although not pink, I do drive an old Cadillac. Granted, it's not the ideal vehicle for a part-time private investigator, but the windows are tinted and it's roomy enough—both key ingredients to a successful surveillance. And for picking up chicks.

I parked along a curb in front of a massive colonial home. Next to the curb was a sign that read: *Tow Away After 8 p.m.* I checked my watch. 2:33 PM. I liked my chances.

The home was near the Sunset Strip, just around the corner from a night club called the Key Club. Been there a few times myself to watch some of the local rock bands. You can take the man out of rock, but you can't take the rock out of the man. Sometimes on Monday nights, from the back of the club, nursing a beer, I watched the lead singer of Metal Skool entertain the frenzied young females with his gyrating hips. There was a time when I would have been arrested for such gyrations. He could thank me later.

The morning sky was overcast and threatened rain. Perhaps the sky would have felt more threatening if this hadn't been L.A. I've lived here for nearly thirty years and still can't get used to the perpetual sunshine. Granted, I liked the sunshine, and it had done wonders for my health, but I was still a sucker for some good old-fashioned gray skies.

The colonial house, complete with Corinthian pillars and alabaster lions, was massive and brooding. The front lawn was manicured to perfection.

As I approached the house, a deep-throated dog began barking. And with each step that I took, the dog's barking grew louder and more frequent. As if on cue. I looked around and didn't see any dog—nothing in the front windows, and nothing along the side of the house. *Maybe it's inside and can sense me. Or smell me.* Either way, it sounded big and vicious and I kept my eyes peeled.

As I crunched up the crushed seashell drive, apprehension crackled through me, and it had nothing to do with the dog. Indeed, it was an old fear born from years of living in hiding, or living on the run, so to speak. *Would this be the person who finally sees through my disguise, see beyond my reconstructed face, and sees the real me? Would this be the moment when my cover is finally blown?*

Crazy, I know, but the fear was real, and it lived within me.

The drastic plastic surgery was, of course, nearly foolproof. Nearly. Still, the apprehension persisted.

And so what if I was found out. Would that be so bad?

Probably not. After all, wouldn't I then be able to see my baby girl again? *And why should she want to see you? You faked your death, split, and left her behind.*

Could I make her understand my motives? Hell, did I even understand my motives? And what about the embarrassment of being discovered? Especially the embarrassment of being discovered living in near poverty?

Jesus, it would be off the charts.

Anxiety gripped me again, completely. My throat constricted. I paused there on the driveway and forced myself to take a deep breath. My chest expanded out against my red Hawaiian shirt. I continued breathing deeply, in and out. The faux dog continued barking a steady staccato. I sensed someone watching me through the big bay windows in the front.

In and out. Deep breaths. Better, better.

Heartbeat slowing. Another breath. Calmer. Good, good. *It's going to be all right, big guy. No one's seen through your disguise yet.*

But what about the package yesterday with the Elvis watch?

At the thought of the package, my heart rate picked up again. Blood pounded in my ears. I felt like turning around, going home, and crawling into bed with a six pack of Newcastle. Someone out there *knew*, and they were toying with me.

I hate when that happens.

I looked at the massive home in front of me. A stiff wind rustled my thinning hair. A girl was missing. A young starlet. She needed help. Her family needed help.

Could I be of help? Wasn't I just a washed-up old man?

Yes and no. I had been working as an investigator for many years now. I specialized in finding the missing. I had helped many, many people.

I'll deal with whoever sent the package later. Hell, it's not the first time I've dealt with a stalker. Granted, it's been a while; still, this will be no different. Okay, maybe a little different. There was a lot more on the line this time: My reputation. My identity. My everything.

Deep breaths, big guy. It's going to be okay.

I was going to be okay.

Breathing. Lungs expanding. Heart rate lowering. And the more I was able to control my breathing, the calmer I became.

The sun was shining. The dog was barking, and I was moving forward once again, with some degree of confidence. My disguise would hold and I would see about helping these people and their missing daughter.

I stepped onto the wide wooden veranda and knocked on the front door.

Show time.

CHAPTER ELEVEN

The door opened almost immediately, and a tall woman holding a glass tumbler materialized in the doorway. She was wearing a terrycloth robe and pink slippers.

"You're late," she said.

"Sorry, ma'am."

"You're the investigator, I assume?"

"Yes, ma'am."

"You're awfully polite."

"Yes, ma'am."

"Where you from?" she asked.

"The South, ma'am,"

"Ah," she said, nodding, as if that explained everything.

She was standing in the doorway with her left arm tucked under her right. Her glass tumbler dangled from her right hand. Something clear was inside it, mixed with clinking ice. Lean bicep and tricep muscles rippled under her paper-thin skin. Veins undulated in places most women did not have veins. At least, not in my day. She was tanned beyond reason. Welcome to Hollywood. Somewhere in the massive edifice behind her I heard a vacuum cleaner running. Other than that, total silence. At least the dog had stopped barking.

She continued standing in the doorway. She wasn't sure about me and wasn't sure she wanted to hire me. I knew the drill. I was old. And, in her mind, no doubt too old to do the job. I was used to the drill, and wasn't offended. Well, not that much, anyway.

"You don't really have a dog, do you?" I said.

"What an odd thing to say."

"Only odd if it's not true."

She studied me a moment longer. "It's motion-activated. A security measure installed by my paranoid husband—God rest his soul—a few years ago. It drives me ape shit. How did you know?"

"Because it was driving me ape shit, too."

She smiled. Ah, camaraderie. She was quite a beautiful woman, actually. About twenty years my junior. Her long, slender nose was red. Her cheeks were red. Everything on her face was red and swollen and puffy. Days of crying. Actually, she looked a little like me after days of drinking.

Still, she wasn't impressed enough to let me in. "Clarke said you find missing children," she said.

"I do my best," I said.

"Even adult missing children?"

"Yes," I said. "Even adult missing children."

"Do you have any of your own?"

"Yes."

"Then you know," she said. "Or, you can imagine...." her voice trailed off.

"Yes," I said. "I can imagine the hell you are going through."

"Will you help me find my daughter, Mr. King?"

"I will do everything in my power, ma'am. I promise you. No stone unturned and all that."

She looked at me some more...and a weak smile appeared. "Do I know you? You look familiar."

"I get that a lot. Most people say I remind them of their grandfathers."

"Yes, maybe that's probably it."

"May I come in, ma'am?"

"Please, call me Dana. And, yes, of course, where's my manners?"

She stepped aside and I was finally permitted entry. She closed the door behind me and I followed her through an ornate foyer and into a massive sitting room. Nice place. Back in the day, I could have lived quite well here, thank you very much.

"Would you like something to drink, Mr. King?"

"Coffee would be fine."

She showed me into the sitting room before stepping through an arched doorway and down a hallway. Her feet padded for a while along the polished wooden floor. Long hallway.

The sitting room was cozy. A central hearth dominated the room, surrounded by an elaborate wrought-iron grate in a creeping ivy design. With this being southern California in late March, there was, of course, no fire. But if there had been, it would have been damn cozy. I moved around the room, lightly touching the fine furniture as I went. I stopped in the far corner at an ornate, and slightly abused, Steinway piano. The keys were exposed and I pressed one or two, each sound sending a thrill straight through my soul. My God, I loved music. I believe it's the closest thing humans have to real magic, and I was happy to have contributed to it.

"My mother gave me that piano," Dana said. She was standing in the doorway, holding a silver tray of steaming mugs. "It's been in the family for nearly eighty years. I know it's an eyesore, but I still play it."

"Oh, really," I said, genuinely intrigued. "What can you play?"

"Anything, really. But mostly songs from the fifties and sixties, from my teens."

Do you know any Elvis? I wanted to ask, but didn't.

She set the tray down on the coffee table, then crossed over to the piano, where she sat on the bench. She motioned for me to sit next to her and I did. She absently pressed one or two keys. Somber notes. Our legs touched.

"Do you play an instrument, Aaron? I'm sorry, may I call you Aaron?"

"Yes, of course."

"Please, call me Dana."

"Yes. You said that."

"I'm sorry, I'm not thinking straight these days," she took in some air, doing her best at small talk, "You're from the South, you say?"

"Near there, yes."

"So you're a true Southern gentleman."

"I try."

"And do you play an instrument?"

"Yes, a little guitar." I said, then admitted to something I hadn't admitted to in nearly thirty years. "But mostly I used to sing."

"Oh, really? Where?"

Now my heart was really pounding, but, dammit, it felt good talking about singing again.

"You know, mostly church choir stuff."

"I bet you have a beautiful voice."

"*Had.* That was long ago."

"Perhaps you should take it up again," she said, pressing more keys. "You're never too old, you know."

I smiled. "Perhaps."

CHAPTER TWELVE

We moved over to the couch, Where Dana told me more about her missing daughter, Miranda.

Mother and daughter were inseparable, closer than best friends. Miranda was a rising film star and had just wrapped shooting her fourth movie in New York, which should be out in time for summer. She had lived a charmed life up to this point.

"Do the police have any suspects?" I asked.

"None that I'm aware of. You'll have to ask them."

Dana picked up a metal picture frame and handed it to me. It was her daughter, and she was gorgeous. A spitting image of her mother, only younger and more vibrant. She instantly reminded me of my own daughter.

"Describe the day she went missing," I said to Dana with-out taking my eyes off the picture. "What were you doing?"

"I was home painting, which I do as a sort of hobby, although sometimes I sell them on eBay."

I nodded politely. People ramble, especially under stress.

"Miranda was in and out all day, as usual. Tanning salon, shopping, grabbing some food. I was happy to see it, because she had been moping around here for the past few days prior to that. After-filming blues, I figured, as the movie had wrapped a month or so earlier and I think she was feeling lonely and out-of-touch. The last time I saw her—" Dana paused, sucking some air, willing herself forward, "The last time I saw her she had popped into my art studio upstairs and asked if I wanted anything from Trader Joe's. I barely looked up. I told her no, and then she was gone. Outside, I heard her car start up and leave and I haven't seen or heard from her since."

I nodded sympathetically, looking away from the picture. "When did you suspect something was wrong?"

"I called her two hours later. We almost always keep in close contact with each other, like an old married couple. But she didn't pick up. I tried again twenty minutes later, and then kept on trying until I thought the worst. I think I called the police sometime in the middle of the night."

I waited a few seconds as she gathered herself.

"That was six days ago," she said.

"And what happens when you call her cell phone now?" I asked.

"It goes straight to voicemail. Only now her voicemail is full—mostly with messages from me, sounding more and more hysterical, no doubt."

"Does Miranda have a boyfriend?"

"No, but she had been texting one of her co-stars in her new movie. They seemed to have hit it off rather well."

"Where does he live?"

"New York."

Dana looked like she was on something, and she probably was, and I didn't blame her one bit. Anything to get through this nightmare.

"How long have you been a private investigator?" she asked.

"Thirty years or so."

"What did you do before?"

"Oh, I was in the entertainment industry."

"My daughter's in the entertainment industry."

"I know," I said, and thought: *So is mine.*

"You are older than the other detectives," she said.

"I'm older than most."

She grinned. "But maybe that's a good thing, maybe you can bring your experience to this. Yes, I like that. Instead of worrying about your age, I can focus on your experience. Maybe your age will, in fact, be an asset."

"Sure," I said gently.

She was nodding vigorously, as if she had just discovered the key that could unlock this whole investigation: an older PI with years of experience behind him.

"Will you help me find her, Mr. King?"

"So I'm hired?"

"Yes, of course."

"Then, I will do everything in my power to bring her home," I said.

Her emotions reversed on a dime. Now she sank in on herself. Literally. She instantly looked deflated and withered, like a plant without water. A mother without her daughter. She sat there on the couch looking at me, her chin pressing against her sternum, her head too heavy to support.

"I'd like to see her room now," I said.

Dana nodded and showed me the way up.

CHAPTER THIRTEEN

I followed her up a wide curving staircase, moving past a great expanse of wall which was covered in family portraits. Ever alert for clues, I studied closely as we ascended.

There was a wedding portrait of a younger version of Dana, looking beautiful and radiant and far too tan. She was hanging happily onto the arm of a dark-haired, bright-eyed young man dressed to the nines in a spiffy tux. I assumed this to be her deceased husband. More pictures of the newlyweds and some family members no doubt long since departed, and then the upper half of the wall, as we continued up, was completely dominated by Miranda in various stages of growing up. There was Miranda missing a tooth, with eyes so big to seem almost unreal, and one of the cutest, roundest faces I'd ever seen. Destined to be a star. Miranda in the Girl Scouts. Miranda riding a horse. Miranda on a class field trip, already head and shoulders cuter than any of the other kids. Miranda in junior high and beginning to look like a young lady. Miranda in high school, but now the cute little girl was gone as she began blossoming into the striking woman she would soon become.

The pictures tapered off, and we presently reached the upstairs landing. Dana led me down a surprisingly narrow hallway, made even more narrow by the placement of bookshelves and small ornate tables. Expensive-looking vases filled with fresh flowers adorned the tables. Or rather, upon second glance, they had been fresh a few days ago. Now they were wilted. She stopped at the last door to the right.

"Here it is," she said. "Take as long as you need."

"Has anyone else been through this room?" I asked.

"Yes, the police."

"And no one since?"

"No."

She looked up at me some more, her eyes searching my face, and I saw the profound depth of her desperation and pain. She nodded for reasons known only to her, then turned and went back down the hallway and on down the stairs.

I let myself into Miranda's bedroom.

CHAPTER FOURTEEN

Fresh air and warm sunshine poured in through the open bedroom window. The room itself was large and bright and cheery. No clothes were strewn across the floor, no jeans draped over the backs of sitting chairs. Nothing was knocked over or spilled. Someone had tidied the place up. I had known a few starlets in my day. Their rooms didn't look like this.

The fresh air was also suffused with a combination of lotions, sprays, ointments and whatever else it took to look glamorous in Hollywood today.

Dominating the room was a four-poster bed with sheer gossamer curtains, pulled back and tied with red velvet ropes. The first thing I did was cross the room and heft the mattress. Nothing underneath. No revealing Polaroids. Not even a pea. I haphazardly poked the sheets back into place, and moved on.

Next was an antique vanity desk with a hand-carved ornate mirror and matching stool. A neat row of cut glass bottles lined the base of the mirror. I opened the vanity's three tiny drawers. The first two were empty, and the third contained an expired driver's license. I studied it. Younger, perhaps just out of high school, very pretty. I put it back, shaking my head.

Don't hate me because I'm beautiful.

I turned and scanned the room. Against the far wall was a closed door. Like a well-used deer trail through a thicket of forest, the polished wooden floor leading up to it was heavily worn and faded.

Miranda's closet, I presume.

I presumed correctly. Under the inadequate light of a single dusty bulb, a sea of tiny clothing stretched as far as the eye could see. Well, at least as far as these old eyes could see. In actuality, the closet itself was about the size of my bedroom at home—and smelled a whole lot nicer.

I went to work, methodically checking every pocket of every jeans, shirt, slacks, short, dress and things indescribable, at least indescribable to guys like me. I didn't find much. One partially open cough drop, a handful of change, a wadded up five-dollar bill and one bar receipt. I left the cough drops and money behind, but I put the receipt into a pocket of my own. Although I didn't step out of a magical wardrobe, I felt as if I were exiting a fantastical, Narnia-like world of sparkly tops, sparkly blue jeans and sparkly shoes.

Don't knock it. You used to sparkle, too.

Back in the bedroom, I next went to all paintings and pictures hanging on her bedroom walls, checking behind each, hoping for a clue, but finding none.

The final piece of untouched furniture was a cherry wood dresser in the far corner of the room. The top was mostly covered with dozens of picture frames featuring Miranda and many of her friends. Miranda had beautiful friends. Like attracts like. In one of the picture frames—a Minnie Mouse picture frame, in fact—Miranda was smiling for the camera, showing her perfect teeth. Chin slightly dimpled. Light in her eyes. Cheekbones kissed by the gods. A nice picture, certainly, if not for the haunted look in her eyes.

The same look my daughter sometimes had.

I pocketed the small frame to keep for my files. No one would miss it. I next worked my way down through all the dresser drawers, rummaging through shorts and mittens and socks and tank tops and undergarments. I felt each of the socks, looking for anything hidden; nothing. The bottom drawer was empty save for a lacquered cigar box. I lifted it out and cleared a space on top of the shelf and set it down. I opened it. Inside was a ticking Minnie Mouse watch and dozens and dozens of love letters, many dating back to what would have been

Miranda's high school years, which, if my math was correct, would have pre-dated text messaging.

I read through some of them since Miranda's privacy had disappeared the moment *she* disappeared. Most of the letters were written by a kid named Flip. Yeah, *Flip*. Apparently he and Miranda had been an item back in the day. A clue? Maybe, maybe not. At any rate, I rummaged through the letters until I found one with the kid's last name on it. Flip Barowski. I confiscated it and a couple of others, tucking them behind the picture frame in my back pocket.

I was just putting the cigar box away in the bottom drawer when a voice spoke behind me.

"I can assure you, Mr. King, that you won't find Miranda in there."

Dana was standing in the doorway. I stood, perhaps a little too quickly. Immediately lightheaded, I steadied myself on the dresser.

"No, ma'am, I don't suppose I would."

"But you're very thorough, I'll give you that."

"You're paying me to be thorough."

She frowned at that, but said, "I have guests arriving soon, Mr. King. Will you be much longer?"

I scanned Miranda's bedroom a final time. The afternoon sun was angling down through the western window. Dust motes caught some of the sunlight, flaring brilliant and then disappearing. Other than her love for clothing and maybe even Flip, nothing else stood out, nothing tell-tale.

I hate when that happens.

I turned back to Dana, who was watching me closely with bloodshot eyes. Her pain was real and her hurt was deep, but I couldn't help but wonder why she was hurrying me along.

"No," I said. "I'm done here."

She showed me down the hallway and down the stairs and then through the front door, which she shut quietly behind me. I stood there a moment on the front porch and sensed her presence just behind me. I think I heard her weeping, but I couldn't be sure since I had activated the faux dog alarm again.

I moved down the crushed shell drive, got in my car and drove around the block and parked further down the road with a clear view of Dana's big house. I waited an hour but no guests arrived.

Maybe they were late.

CHAPTER FIFTEEN

Kelly and I were in Best Buy looking at a lot of stuff I couldn't afford. I was hoping to get a new printer, but I wasn't liking the prices. Luckily, there was always Craigslist.

"I could buy you a new printer, you know," said Kelly, holding my hand. "We can call it an early birthday present."

"Thank you, but no thank you."

"You're a stubborn bastard."

"It's called being old-fashioned."

"But I make more money than you, and I want to help you. What's wrong with that?"

"Nothing, but that's where the old-fashioned part comes in."

"You can't let a woman buy you something that you need."

"Something like that," I said.

"The guy is supposed to be strong, the provider."

"You got it."

"Even when the provider hasn't done much providing, even for himself."

"Even then," I said.

"I think it's just silly pride," said Kelly.

"Silly pride is all I have left," I said.

We were now strolling through the TV section, admiring big screen TVs that looked wider than my apartment wall, and clearer than my windows. I should really clean my windows.

And that's when I heard it. One of my old songs. Hearing an old song of mine, anywhere, always had an effect on me. And what sort of effect depended on my mood. If I was feeling happy and at peace with the world, hearing one of my old songs always put a smile on my face and reminded me of the good ole days. If I was in a shitty mood, hearing one of my old songs was the absolute last thing I wanted to hear. And, apparently, this Elvis chap was everywhere, and so it was a rare day that I wasn't reminded of my past.

In this particular case, I was in a fairly lukewarm state of mind. Sure, Kelly and I had been snipping a little at each other, but it was all in good fun. And, sure, my finances weren't exactly where I wanted them to be, but I wasn't particularly stressed over it; at least, not at the present. The song, however, didn't appear to be coming from over the store's speakers, and so I took Kelly's hand, searching for the source.

And what I found was highly unexpected.

I had heard of *Rock Band* and *Guitar Hero*, of course. Any musician in the industry would have immediately taken note of popular video games that feature rock bands and rock songs.

Not too many things surprised me these days, but I was, admittedly, surprised to see this.

"Elvis Presley: Rock Band," said Kelly, picking up a box and examining the back of it. "Cute."

Three kids were crowded around the game, although only one seemed to be actually demoing it. By demoing, I mean he was using a plastic guitar and rapidly pressing various buttons built into the guitar's fretboard, all while a computer generated image of the King of Rock, Elvis Presley himself, sang "Jailhouse Rock" in front of a screaming, raucous crowd. On one side of the screen, multi-colored notes appeared and disappeared. I assumed the colors were associated with the colored buttons on the fretboard. No doubt the object of the game was to press the buttons in conjunction with the appearance of the musical notes, in a simulation of playing a real guitar.

I found it fascinating, perhaps even more fascinating because the game featured *my music*. No doubt the royalties off this game alone would set me up for the rest of my life.

Dead men don't get royalties.

True enough, and dead men can't sue, either. Years ago, just prior to faking my death, I had set aside a small fortune to live off comfortably. That small fortune disappeared quickly, due in part to my own poor judgment and to outright theft by my money handlers. The money handlers hadn't been privy to my hoax and had promptly raided my account with news of my alleged death. With most of my money gone, I was soon forced to find real work; in particular, work that had *nothing* to do with the music industry. I answered an ad in the want-ads and soon ended up working for a local private investigator. The work was fun and challenging and I decided to keep at it. When the time came for me to get my P.I. license—and thus get fingerprinted—I had only mild concerns that the prints would come back belonging to one Elvis Aaron Presley, deceased. Back in 1977, when I had had my massive face-altering plastic surgery, I also had the prints from all ten digits shuffled around. The procedure throws off most fingerprint databases and, luckily, it had thrown off the Department of Justice's database back in the early '80s, too. My ruse worked, and I was given my investigator's license.

Now, as I watched the kid rock out to one of my own songs, I could give a shit about all the royalties I was missing out on. All I wanted to do was play, too.

Kelly tugged on my arm to get us moving again, but I told her to hold on. She said fine and wandered off to look around.

When "Jailhouse Rock" came to an end, and the on-screen Elvis avatar bowed to the screaming crowd, the kid playing the game turned to one of his friends and said, "Beat that, bitch!"

The pull was too great. The chance to play one of my own songs and watch a computer generated image of me on-screen, was just too cool to pass up. I stepped forward, "Actually, do you mind if this old bitch has a try at it?"

One of the kids laughed, maybe at my joke, maybe at me. Or both. The one playing the game shrugged and handed me the fake guitar and even showed me how to use it. He next started a new game for me, or a new song, and before I knew it, the computerized Elvis, circa

1968, was back on stage. Kelly, appearing like a groupie, was by my side again, shaking her head and grinning. "Why am I not surprised?" she said. "You always had a thing for Elvis."

"Maybe it's a man-crush," I said.

On the big screen in front of me, notes appeared and disappeared, traveling along a sort of blue highway and coming at me rapidly. I looked from the screen to my hand, and tried pressing the corresponding colored button.

"Too late," said the kid helping me. "You have to press them sooner, as soon as they appear."

I nodded, getting it. The other kid laughed again as I missed the next few notes, too. Hell, even the computerized crowd started booing.

"Just ignore them," said the first kid. "You'll get it."

He explained further: When the note reached the bottom of the screen, I was also to use the plastic strum bar, and for each successive note, strum again, using the music's beat and melody to help me gauge when to play.

Easy, right? No. The game, although simple enough, required ludicrously dexterous fingers. Perhaps too dexterous for my old hands, but I wanted to give it a shot.

After all, these were *my* songs, right?

After a few more seconds of failure, and laughing from the other kid, I eventually associated the colored buttons to my matching fingers. Playing the thing was all about rhythm and muscle memory, and luckily I had plenty of rhythm—and even some ancient muscle memory stored away in my old fingers. After all, I had played real guitars on real stages to these very songs.

The plastic guitar had a nice feel to it. I hadn't held a guitar in decades, but this was already bringing back old memories. Fond memories. Damn good memories, in fact.

"Hey, you're getting it," said the first kid.

"Not bad," said Kelly, nudging me with her elbow. "At least the crowd quit booing."

Now the song picked up in temp, and the notes and colors came at me faster and faster. My fingers, now fully warmed up, flew over the colored key pad. I strummed when I was supposed to. I could almost—*almost*—imagine being back on stage and doing this for real.

More kids had come up to watch. The one who had been laughing wasn't laughing any more. My fingers, I knew, were a blur. My advantage was easy: I knew this song in my sleep. Hell, I knew the notes and chords in my sleep, too, even after all these years.

A couple of Best Buy workers came over as well, and now I heard people whispering behind me. I heard the first kid tell them that I had never played before. Someone else said, "No way."

Yes way, I thought.

I blocked them all out and finished the song in a flourish, strumming and pressing buttons so fast that I knew my fingers would be swollen and sore for days or weeks to come. And when the song was over, when the last button had been pressed, I realized I was gasping for breath and holding the guitar out in front of me as I had done countless times on stage. Sweat was on my brow; I might have been dancing, too, but I couldn't recall. I had been, as they say, in the zone and oblivious to those around me.

When I opened my eyes and settled back on planet earth, the first kid who helped me was staring up at me in disbelief. Everyone, in fact, was staring at me. Even Kelly. Their faces ranged from humor to surprise.

I handed the guitar back to the kid, who was still staring me. "What?" I asked him.

"You were playing with your eyes closed," he said.

"Probably not a good thing, huh?"

"But you scored perfectly, hitting every note, without looking. It was incredible."

I grinned. "Sometimes you get lucky."

CHAPTER SIXTEEN

I was at a bar called Skippers in Hollywood, drinking Newcastle straight from the bottle and, thanks to a handful of Vicodins, working on one hell of a good buzz.

Booze and Vicodins. Don't try this at home, kids.

Normally, I take about five a day, but lately I've been noticing the effects were not the same. Not as strong. I felt good, sure, but not great, and sometimes the aches and pains came back sooner than anticipated.

Can't have that.

Nope.

Maybe I should start taking six or seven a day.

The idea appealed immensely. I reached inside my jacket pocket, found the bottle of Vicodins, popped the cap with my thumb, shook two more pills out and clicked the cap back on. All with one hand, a real pro at this stuff. Something I'm not necessarily proud of. Anyway, I knocked them back with a beer chaser.

Okay, so now we're officially up to seven a day. Two weeks ago I had gone from four to five. Now it's five to seven.

I'm making bigger jumps.

Ten minutes later the prescription drugs were having the desired effect. Blessed numbness, followed by a stronger than normal buzz thanks to the beer. Suddenly, the stool I was sitting on didn't seem very stable. Maybe it was lopsided.

Funny, it wasn't lopsided when you first sat down.

No. It wasn't.

Seven Vicodins was a lot. Too many. And soon even that amount wouldn't be enough, would it? Soon I would be up to ten, fifteen, twenty. But you don't care, do you? Because you feel good now. You feel good and pain-free and life isn't so miserable because of the Vicodins.

Fuck the Vicodins.

Okay, I didn't mean that.

I drank some more beer and removed the framed photograph from my pocket. It was Miranda, of course, and she was staring back at me with a twinkle in her eye, a half-smile on her lips, her cheekbones high, her hair a flowing glossy wave of black. She was wearing an open-neck white blouse, and I saw behind the half smile. I saw an insecure little girl who still loved Minnie Mouse.

I took another drink and continued staring at the picture and thought of my own daughter again. And again.

And again....

"Is she your daughter?" asked the bartender. He was an older man with a thick mustache.

"Not quite," I said.

He grinned easily. "She's very beautiful," he said.

"Yes, she is."

At the back of the bar, near a small stage, there was some activity. I'm always on the lookout for stages. Call it a habit. Someone was setting up a karaoke machine.

Oh, goody.

The bartender moved away. I turned back to the picture, drank some more beer. Someone spoke into a microphone, testing it. Ten minutes later, someone else was singing something by Tom Petty. I liked Tom Petty. Ugly as sin, but I like him.

No one followed the Tom Petty act, and so the karaoke DJ filled the lull by singing "Love Me Tender" by Elvis Presley.

And butchered the hell out of it.

Disgusted, I set a twenty on the table and tried to stand but somehow tripped over the wobbly stool. I fell hard and loudly. The bartender was instantly by my side.

"Let me call you a cab, pal," he said, helping me to my feet. "Or you can cool off over there." He pointed to some seats in front of the stage and motioned to the singer. "He sounds alright after a few beers."

I said something derogatory under my breath. Apparently, I wasn't a good judge of volume these days.

The bartender laughed. "Well, guy, if you think you can do better, why don't you give it a shot? Would probably clear your head a little."

"No...I can't," I said.

"Why not?"

"I don't sing anymore." The last time I sang was for little Beth Ann, but I was not yet in the habit of breaking out in song, especially when drunk.

"Anymore? So you used to?"

I hesitated. "Yes."

"C'mon. Let's sober you up." He took my arm and guided me through the mostly empty bar, and up onto the small karaoke stage. The DJ was still singing—and still butchering.

"Here's one for you, Rick," said the bartender.

Rick nodded and, still singing, found an extra microphone and tossed it over to me. Except I saw *three* microphones. I swiped at the middle one, and missed. Someone in the crowd laughed. Rick, without missing a beat, picked it up and wrapped my hands securely around it. He smiled encouragingly. The small crowd clapped encouragingly. Hell, I was encouraged. But I was also nearly drunk.

I looked dumbly at the microphone. I hadn't held a microphone in years. Decades.

I swallowed hard.

"Love Me Tender" was still pumping through the speakers. Suddenly, I no longer cared that Rick had sounded bad.

I continued staring at the microphone. The crowd clapped louder. Rick nudged me, trying to catch my eye, but I couldn't tear my gaze away from the object in my hand.

The microphone.

The song continued playing. Rick continued butchering.

Rick gave up on me and moved to the opposite side of the stage, distancing himself from the drunk old man. He must have said something or gestured toward me, because there was a smattering of laughter.

Laughing at me.

I stared at the microphone.

The song ended and Rick put a gentle hand on my elbow and guided me off the stage and back to a booth. There I sat until I sobered, and while I sobered all I could think about was how perfect and natural the microphone had felt in my hand.

CHAPTER SEVENTEEN

I was in Detective Colbert's office. We were both drinking Starbucks coffee from paper cups. The paper cups were wrapped with a thickish sort of brown sleeve.

"Here's a question for you, King," said Colbert. "Why don't these cups start with the cardboard sleeve, rather than slipping them on later?"

"As in built in?"

"Yeah, that's it, built in."

"Makes too much sense," I said.

He nodded. "Nothing much makes sense in that place."

"Nope."

"How much did these two coffees cost you?" he asked.

"I bought a scone, too," I said.

"What the fuck is a scone?"

"It's Irish, I think, for stale bread."

"So how much for two large coffees and a scone?"

"Twelve bucks," I said. "And some change."

"If you were trying to bribe me, King," said Colbert. "Just give me the twelve bucks and change."

"It's illegal to bribe a cop."

He held up his coffee. "What do you call this?"

"Damn expensive coffee."

"Exactly. So what do you need, King? You don't just show up here with coffee worth its weight in gold for nothing."

"I'm working on the Miranda Scott case."

Colbert was a small man with a thick neck. His fingers were short and blunt, which often made for the best fists. Those fingers were now laced around the coffee's protective cardboard sleeve, safe from the heat within. He snorted.

"You're the third private dick to come in here about this case, King. I happen to be a busy man, you know."

"If you were any busier," I said, "you would be a blur."

He searched absently for the tiny hole in the lid, found it and sipped. "Fucking thing's not even hot," he said.

He pulled off the sleeve and tossed it in the wastebasket under his desk.

"Almost seems naked," I said. "Without the sleeve."

Colbert sat back and looked at me. "You come in here bribing me with cold coffee and insulting my investigative techniques." He shook his head. "It's a good thing I like you, King."

"What's not to like?"

"Your accent, for one. How long you fucking been in California?"

"Nearly thirty years."

"And yet you still sound like you should be calling pigs."

"It's my Southern charm."

He sipped some more coffee, turned in his chair and looked out over Los Angeles. We were on the fifth floor of LAPD's downtown office. A chopper flew past the window, catching some of the bright afternoon sun. Colbert inhaled deeply. Not quite a sigh. He was too tough to sigh.

"We have nothing," he said. "And if we had something, that would be twice as much as we have now."

"Which is nothing."

"You got it."

"No leads?" I asked.

"Only one. A neighbor saw a white van parked along the street on the day she went missing."

"Plates?"

"Nope."

"Description of the driver?"

"Caucasian male. And that's it."

"No one approached him?" I asked.

"Nope; he was simply observed."

"And that's it?" I said.

"So far. We're following up with everyone she'd ever known. But no one can explain why she didn't come home from Trader Joe's or where she could be now. From all appearances, she's disappeared off the face of the earth."

"A random kidnapping?"

He shrugged. He still wasn't looking at me. Cops didn't like private investigators as a general rule. Which is why I played the kindly old man card and brought the coffee and tried not to trample on toes. I needed him, and I needed to know what stones had been turned.

"Maybe," he said. "Hard to say. Maybe she just ran away."

"She just finished filming a movie," I said. "She presumably has a lot to live for. This is a very exciting time in her life. Why would she run away now?"

"Maybe she cracked under the pressure," said Colbert.

"Being an actress is her life's dream."

"So then maybe she's celebrating in Hawaii with her co-stars and didn't bother to tell dear old mom."

"Except she tells her mother everything."

"You think she's telling her mom about every guy she fools around with?"

"Doesn't everyone?"

He shook his head. "I still think she's out partying somewhere. Vegas maybe. She'll show up."

"Or not."

He studied me a moment. "You're here for the file," he said. He stretched his short legs under his desk and crossed his ankles. He didn't look like a man who was looking very hard for a missing girl. Maybe his instincts were right and mine were wrong.

"Well," I said. "Maybe just a peek."

"You promise to stay out of my hair?"

"I work on my own," I said. "I happen to be a helluva self-starter."

He thought about it, nodded. "You have a bit of a reputation for finding people. You could, of course, just be damn lucky."

"There's always that."

"Either way, we could use the help." He slid a manila file toward me. "Make a copy of this. Tell no one. Bosses don't like us giving away our real police work to private dicks."

"Sure thing."

"And King?"

"Yeah?"

"Anyone ever mention you sound like Elvis?"

I took the file and stood. "Once or twice."

CHAPTER EIGHTEEN

It was after hours, and I was sitting in the Trader Joe's manager's office. By "office" I meant a raised platform at the front of the store. I think the openness of the manager's office was supposed to inspire a sense of trust and togetherness with the employees and customers. I thought it inspired a sense of opportunity for thieves. Then again, what did I know? I'm just a simple private dick.

The Trader Joe's store manager was a thin man with pale skin. Since there was absolutely nothing remarkable or distinguishing about him, I decided he needed a tattoo. Or a piercing. Something, anything to distinguish him. His name was Ernie.

"Look," Ernie was saying, "I'm sorry to sound rude, but I've been through this at least a dozen times now. I don't know what else to say that hasn't already been said before."

"I understand," I said. People like Ernie shut doors. People like me opened them. That is, when I'm sober. "Does anyone from your staff remember seeing her?"

Behind me, the closed grocery store was a beehive of activity as employees swept and stocked and cleaned.

"Christ, have you ever been here during rush hour?" he asked.

"Like Pamplona," I said, "minus the bulls."

He didn't find me very funny. "I'm sorry, Mr. King, but no one remembers seeing her."

That wasn't entirely true. According to the police report, which I had committed to memory after many careful readings, a young employee working in the parking lot *had* reported seeing her. Ernie wasn't being entirely honest with me. I wondered why. Maybe he was just eager to tally up that day's receipts and go home. Maybe.

"Is Edward Rutherford here tonight?" I asked.

Ernie knew he was caught. "You know about Ed?" he asked.

"Yup," I said.

The store manager drummed his fingers on his desk. "Look, I just want this to go away. I've had police investigators in and out of here for the past week, not to mention a handful of you private eye guys, or whatever it is you call yourselves."

"I prefer investigative engineer."

But he wasn't listening to me. "Anyway, it's been totally disruptive. I should be counting registers right now, but instead I'm dealing with this again."

"It's very inconvenient," I said, "when someone disappears."

"Hell, yes, it's inconvenient."

"It's probably less inconvenient than being kidnapped and murdered."

"Nobody said anything about a murder."

"No, not yet," I said. "But it's looking more and more probable. And it happened on *your* store's property. Imagine how that's going to play out once word gets out. Talk about your PR problems, Ernie. You think investigators are harsh? Wait until *Access Hollywood* gets wind of this."

The color drained from his face, and kept on draining until he was as white as snow. "We need to find her," he finally said.

"I couldn't agree more," I said.

"I'll go get Edward."

"Good idea."

CHAPTER NINETEEN

Edward was a lanky kid wearing badly faded jeans, a red Hawaiian shirt, and a dour expression. I introduced myself and told him why I was here. He shrugged; obviously, he was overjoyed. I asked if he could show me where he had seen Miranda on the evening of her disappearance. He shrugged again and nodded.

"Over here," he said in a monotone. He led the way through the automatic front doors, which Ernie had left unlocked for us, and out across the mostly empty parking lot.

Trader Joe's isn't a big market, but it attracted big business. The small parking lot, which wrapped all the around to the rear of the store, was often packed to overflowing with vehicles, with many more squatting for a parking space to open up.

Edward led me past a long row of red plastic shopping carts and hung a right, leading us to a section of parking lot located behind the store. Now behind the building, he pointed to the second to last parking spot, to an area that abutted a gently rising dirt hill.

"I saw her park here."

I nodded. According to the police file, this was indeed where Miranda's vehicle had been discovered. So far so good. Still, I wasn't learning anything new.

I continued scanning the back lot. Three cars were presently parked back here, one of which was quite dusty and appeared abandoned. Opposite the parking lot was the store's receiving docks. The docks were stacked with empty wooden pallets, with broken shopping carts parked haphazardly about. Two Dumpsters were packed to overflowing with straining trash bags and flattened cardboard boxes. A homeless woman was sleeping between the two Dumpsters. It looked kinda cozy, actually.

"What do you do here at Trader Joe's?" I asked Edward.

He shrugged. "I'm a box boy."

I detected a noticeable lack of pride in his voice.

"You bag groceries inside?" I asked.

"Yes."

"But you saw her park her car outside?"

"Yes. Sometimes we take turns collecting shopping carts."

"What time of day did she arrive?"

He thought about it. "I started work at four. This was sometime before my first break. Probably around six."

"Did you also see her leave?" I already knew the answer. According to the police report, Edward had stated he had not seen her leave.

But now he hesitated...and continued hesitating. He looked away and bit his lip. Ah. Something that *wasn't* in the police report, perhaps?

"Well, I was bagging groceries when she left. I might have seen her leave, but I'm not sure. You know, we're pretty busy at that time."

"So I've heard," I said. "But you did see her leave, didn't you, Edward?"

He didn't answer me. He was looking off somewhere in the near or far distance, hard to tell at night. He sucked in some air to speak, but remained silent.

"Look, you did nothing wrong," I said. "Most of the men in your store were probably checking her out. Nothing wrong with that. You're only human."

He nodded; we were silent some more, then he said, "Is this just between you and me?"

"I don't see anyone else around, except for that old lady sleeping between the Dumpsters, but I'm pretty sure she's high or drunk or waiting for her boyfriend Ernie to get off work."

Edward laughed, but he still wasn't talking.

"What do you know, Edward?" I pressed.

"It could be nothing," he finally said.

"*Could be* is more than what we have now."

"It's just a hunch," he said.

"I live and die by hunches."

"I didn't tell the police—" He paused.

"Because you didn't want them to know that you were secretly watching her."

He took another deep breath. Like pulling teeth, this one. Finally, he said, "There was a guy, a bum. He was watching her, too."

My pulse quickened. In the hills above, tree branches rustled in the breeze. Lights in the houses twinkled, appearing and disappearing behind the shifting branches.

"How do you know he was a bum?"

"I've seen him outside before, begging for money."

"Okay, so he was a bum. Lots of people were watching her, Edward, we established that."

"I know."

"Besides, you were busy and didn't see her leave, right?"

"Yeah, I know," he said, "but when I looked up again, she was gone…and so was he. I'm pretty sure he followed her out."

"Okay," I said, taking a deep breath of my own. "Tell me about him."

And so he did.

CHAPTER TWENTY

"So why didn't this Edward kid tell the police about the bum?" asked Kelly, my on-again/off-again girlfriend.

We were in my apartment cooking a late-night dinner together. I'm not much of a cook, granted, but I've developed a few specialties. One of them is spaghetti, which is what we were cooking now. At the moment, the spaghetti was boiling but the pasta was still hard and translucent and not very appetizing. Soon that would all change. Ah, the magic of spaghetti.

"And admit he was following her?" I asked. "Stalking her in his own way, however innocent it might have been? That could look bad."

"So why not make something up?" she asked.

"And lie to the police? Bad things happen when you lie to the police, especially if you're not very good at it."

"So why does he spill his guts to you?"

"I'm not the police. He felt comfortable around me. And, I believe, he was feeling guilty."

"Guilty?" she said.

"Guilty because the information he held back might have helped find her."

"So he tells you now after, what, almost a week?"

"Better late than never," I said.

"But the little shit might have waited too long."

Kelly was still dressed in a cream-colored power suit, having come straight from a meeting with some high-level executive types at Paramount Studios. She thought the suit made her look fat. I thought the suit made her look yummy. She didn't care what I thought. As she sipped from her wineglass, she left behind a very sexy lipstick smudge on the rim.

"So what will you do with this info?" she asked.

"Find the bum, talk to him."

"You think the bum did something to her?"

"I don't know," I said.

"And how will you find him? We are, after all, talking about a bum."

I grinned. "I'll figure something out. I am, after all, an ace detective."

"Or so you keep telling me."

I stirred the boiling spaghetti, which was softening and turning more opaque. Doing its own kind of magic.

Kendra the Wonder Kat was sitting on top of the refrigerator, watching the whole show below, her whiskers occasionally twitching, her glowing yellow eyes alert should I accidentally open a can of tuna and place it in front of her.

"Kendra worships you," said Kelly.

"She has to worship me," I said, adding a touch of salt. "I feed her."

Kelly was seated on a stool, elbows on the Formica breakfast counter, which, at the moment, was doubling as a bar counter. The bar counter sort of hovered over my kitchen sink, allowing her full view of my every move. Lucky girl. She was currently snacking on some leftover corn chips from Tito's Tacos and drinking from her third glass of white wine. Her eyes had that glazed look they get when she's nearly drunk.

"You're quite graceful, Aaron King, when you want to be. Are you sure you weren't a dancer in a past life?"

"I'm sure."

"How come we never go out dancing?"

"I'm too old to dance. I might break a hip or something."

She grinned and drank some more wine, then hummed a little song to herself. "Rubbernecking" by one Elvis Aaron Presley. One of my favorites. I stirred the spaghetti. It was looking more and more whitish, and thus more and more appetizing.

"So what do you think happened to this girl?" asked Kelly.

"I think something very bad happened to this girl."

"Can you help her?"

"As best as I can."

"And your best...."

"Is pretty damn good," I finished.

"You're going to find her, aren't you?"

"Dead or alive," I said.

I poured the spaghetti into a colander, drained it, then dumped the steaming heap of noodles into a large plastic bowl. The spaghetti was white and plump and looked nothing like it had just a few minutes earlier.

"Like magic," I said. "Hard and turgid one minute, soft and supine the next."

"You do realize that we're talking about spaghetti here, right?"

"Yes."

"Seven-year-olds can make spaghetti."

"No," I said. "They can make *magic*."

CHAPTER TWENTY-ONE

"Let's talk about your deceased brother," said Dr. Vivian.
"I never had a brother," I said.
"But you did," she said softly. "For nine months, in the womb, you had a twin brother."

It was just past nine o'clock in the morning. The sunlight was shining through the partially open blinds. This time there was no cat and bird high drama. At least, not yet.

I said, "I see you've been doing your research."
"As have you, Mr. King."
"What do you mean?"

She sat back. "I specialize in twin research. You knew that, which is undoubtedly why you picked me to be your therapist."

"I picked you because you're cuter than sin."

She ignored that. "Further, you probably know that I'm a twin myself. As were you."

Indeed I was. For nine months, like she said. Suddenly I could barely speak. "But he was born dead," I said.

"But he was alive with you in the womb. For nine months he was alive and you had yourself a twin brother."

I found myself staring out the window, through the partially open blinds, at a gently swaying tree branch. I locked onto it, watching its every movement, absorbing its every detail. As I did so, I could hear my own heart beating, loudly and powerfully in my chest. And as I meditated on the branch and lost myself to its texture and movements, as I listened to my own heart beating steadily in my chest, I heard something else. Something not entirely unexpected.

After all, I had heard it before.

It was another heartbeat, a *tiny* heartbeat, and it rose up through the ages, up through the depths of my soul, up through my subconscious. Demanding to be heard.

And it wasn't my own.

It was the heartbeat of someone who had been very close to me. The heartbeat of someone who had been stolen away from me. The heartbeat of someone I had never had the pleasure to know.

Dr. Vivian was watching me. I could feel those big eyes of hers on me. But she said nothing, letting me work through whatever issues her words had stirred within me. The branch outside the window waved gently, sometimes even scraping the exterior of the house, and even the window itself, creating a grating, high-pitched sound on par with fingernails on a chalkboard.

Dr. Vivian eased forward. "How do you feel about losing your twin brother, Mr. King?"

I sucked in some air and my eyes stung with a thin coat of salty tears. "I think it's a damn shame the little guy never met his ma," I said.

She was quiet, but the tree branch wasn't. For now, it continued grating, scraping, the sound of it filling the small office, momentarily blocking out the tiny heartbeats in my head.

I said, "I think it's a damn shame that while I was in the hospital with her, he was being buried on some hillside, left alone to rot in the cold and dirt and emptiness."

Dr. Vivian didn't move.

"I think it's a damn shame he never got to play with me, or laugh with me, or grow up with me, or...."

Words failed me. Tears blurred my vision.

"Or sing with you," she finished, somehow reading my thoughts.

"Yes, ma'am," I said. "I think...I think I would have very much liked to sing with my older brother, Jessie. He was born first you know. He was my older brother, and I think he would have had a damn fine voice."

"How much older was he?"

"Thirty minutes," I said. "And they say he never took even a single breath."

"Do you blame the doctors for not saving him?"

"The doctor was a good man. Knowing Jessie was probably lost, he was more concerned about saving me."

"And what if you had been born first?" she asked quietly.

"Then it would have been me up there on that hill, ma'am," I said. "And if my brother had a chance to live, he might have done things differently. He might have been a wonderful father and a wonderful husband, and he might not have ruined his life."

"You feel guilty for living?"

"Hard not to," I said.

"Because Jessie might have done things differently?"

"No. Because Jessie might have done things *better*."

CHAPTER TWENTY-TWO

As a light rain pleasantly tapped my sliding glass door, with a cold beer in hand, I pressed the "Play" button on my DVD remote control and settled in to watch a movie called "Some *Don't* Like it Hot".

Catchy.

It was Miranda's first movie, made back when she was eighteen-years-old, and fresh off the boat, so to speak. It was about a gang of bank robbers who disguise themselves as women, and end up kidnapping a female bank employee during their escape. The employee is, of course, Miranda, and those in the gang invariably vie for her affections, all while on the run from the law.

Two hours and a six-pack of beer later, I slipped in movie #2, called "The Shallows". This one was a suspense thriller, and a little too violent for my tastes. In it, Miranda plays a character kidnapped by a serial killer and forced to live in his basement, where she comes oh-so-close to escape, only to be killed after a botched police rescue.

Three shots of whiskey later and I was on to her third movie, and quickly losing my ability to grasp plots. This one seemed to be about a College frat party gone wrong. Or right, depending on how you looked at it. There were lots of breasts and farm animals and far too many hairy guys for my liking. Although she didn't have much to work with, Miranda played her part admirably, and in the end the nerd in the group somehow managed to win her affections by besting the jock in a game of poker. Been there, done that.

After six straight hours of mindless nonsense, I finally turned the TV off and staggered to the bathroom. Once done, I plopped down in front of my computer and spent the next two hours looking up everything I could find about Miranda Scott. In the end, after perusing hundreds of articles and dozens of unofficial websites, I was no closer to finding her than when I had started the evening.

But I was thorough, dammit.

Drunk, but thorough.

CHAPTER TWENTY-THREE

It was noon and the day was warm and I was dressed in jeans and a Polo shirt and white sneakers. After a quick stop at the pet supply store for my shiny new crime-fighting tool, I parked my car in the Trader Joe's parking lot, next to the spot where Miranda's car had been found.

I sat in my old car, in the heat, and studied the scene. I knew Miranda's car was now in a police-impound yard, being thoroughly scoured for any forensic evidence. I wished them luck. She had come alone, and left by other means. I was confident her vehicle would turn up nothing, but you never knew. Then again her assailant, for all I knew, had leaned a hand on her hood or inadvertently lost a nose hair. We'll see.

According to the police file, it was unknown what she had purchased that day at Trader Joe's. Her credit card showed no activity, so it was assumed she had paid with cash. Her cell phone records indicated nothing out of the ordinary, although she did place one call to a close female friend about an hour before her trip to the market. That friend, of course, had been thoroughly interviewed, and it turns out the conversation had only lasted three minutes. Just a quick hello call. Miranda's *last* hello call.

So where were the groceries? They hadn't been in or around her car. The car itself had been found locked and secured. Which means she took them with her, wherever she had gone.

Which means she never made it back to her car.

There was an exterior surveillance camera, which was only pointed at the front entrance, and which only Detective Colbert had been privy to. According to the detective, Miranda could be seen entering Trader Joe's through the automatic sliding doors. Nineteen minutes later she is seen leaving alone, exiting with a single bag of groceries. Ten seconds later, a man does indeed follow her out, a tall blond man who may or may not have been a bum. At any rate, the blond man had entered the store about five minutes *prior* to Miranda's arrival, and so the police had dismissed him as a possible suspect, or even a person of interest.

But I knew otherwise. I knew the man was no doubt the same man, the bum, Ed had seen following her around the store, the same guy who had taken a keen interest in her *after* her arrival. He had followed her out, and what happened next I didn't know, except that she had apparently disappeared from the face of the earth.

True, *I* didn't know what happened to her, but I was figuring the bum probably did.

Trader Joe's, at the time of her disappearance, had been damn busy. At that hour cars would have been trawling the parking lot in search of a spot. Having shopped here often myself, I knew the feeling of desperation to find a spot. So, more than likely, she had not been hauled kicking and screaming into some unknown car. There would have been too many witnesses for such a brazen kidnapping.

So what does that mean?

"It means she knew the guy," I said to myself.

How do you know it's a guy?

"Call it a hunch."

No groceries in the car. No keys in the door. No sign of a scuffle. No report of foul play, no report of a girl needing help, and no report of someone being abducted.

Which is why Detective Colbert figured she had split on her own accord, a twenty-two year old runaway.

It was a nice theory and it made his job easier.

But I had a different theory. Then again, my theory was a work in progress.

I stepped out of my car and shut the door behind me. Heat waves rose off the baking pavement. There was no reason to search the crime scene—if it was a crime scene—as it had been thoroughly scoured by the SID investigators; so far, no physical evidence of any type had turned up.

Trader Joe's was quiet at this early hour, an ideal time to shop. I strolled past the long line of grocery carts, crossed in front of the sliding doors, although I didn't go in, and kept going until I was standing on the sidewalk that ran in front of the store. In front of me was a street called Rowena Ave.

Now, if I were a bum, where would I go?

Across the street was another, bigger, grocery store. Although bigger, my impression of it was that it wasn't as popular as the Trader Joe's. I continued scanning. There were three, yes *three*, video rentals stores all within a stone's throw of each other. Grocery stores and video stores, yes. Bums, no. The street, as far as I could tell, was presently bum-free, but that didn't mean they weren't here, somewhere. Hiding. Drinking. Bumming.

Silver Lake is comprised mostly of young Hollywood types. The assistant directors, the TV writers, the up-and coming actors and film students. Young Hollywood aside, the area was not immune to its share of the housing impaired. Hey, if you're gonna go homeless somewhere, might as well do it in southern California, right? Sand, sunshine, and babes. And enough money floating around to keep you fat and happy forever.

The day was warming and the sun was hot on my face. Sweat was building up between my shoulder blades. Any movement at all would probably jiggle the sweat droplets free.

If I were a bum, where would I go?

My scanning eyes found a small, rundown convenience store about a half a block down the street. The hand-painted sign out front read simply: "Liquor". Graffiti covered the wall facing me, and I had no doubt that graffiti covered the other walls, too. A thin black man was hunkered down near a payphone that I seriously doubted worked, and next to him was a full to overflowing shopping cart. Not surprisingly, the shopping cart *wasn't* full to overflowing with groceries.

If I was a bum, I suddenly knew where I would go. A bum-friendly liquor store.

CHAPTER TWENTY-FOUR

The liquor store was in shambles. Dirty floors, narrow aisles, messy shelves. If I owned the place I would be embarrassed. The man behind the counter, a very small, older Korean man, did not appear embarrassed. Instead, he appeared very interested in the newspaper he was reading. Sitting on a shelf behind him was a flickering, black and white, closed-circuit television. Framed within in it, I could see myself standing at the counter, sporting my striking head of gray-brown hair, looking a little heavy. But you know what they say: the camera always adds ten pounds.

I continued standing at the counter and the little man continued reading his paper—and continued not bothering to look up. Probably because I hadn't set anything *on* the counter.

He calmly turned a page.

I cleared my throat. He turned another page. I grabbed a homemade peanut butter cookie wrapped in cellophane and pushed it across the counter. He looked at it. "Two dolla'," he said.

I noticed that the Aaron King standing in the closed-circuit TV screen was looking a bit exasperated. Handsome, granted, but exasperated. I didn't blame him one bit. Two dolla' for a peanut butter cookie was highway robbery. I opened my wallet.

"There's a bum who comes around here," I said.

The clerk turned back to his paper. "Bums always come 'round here."

"This one is tall and blond and sports a ponytail. He usually has a dog with him."

The dog, of course, was the gimmick. Probably tripled the guy's handouts. The clerk looked up from his paper and looked at me for the first time. He grinned. "I think you need one more cookie. You a growing boy."

"Oh, brother," I said.

I slapped a twenty on the counter. He smiled widely and reached for it. "Sure," he said. "He come in here all the time. Buy single malt whiskey. The good stuff. That dog make him lots of money."

"He ever buy anything for the dog?"

"It look like I sell dog food?"

"Good point," I said. "When did you last see him?"

"One hour ago."

My pulse quickened. "Any idea where he went?"

"You think I know where every bum go?"

"Fine," I said. "Can you at least point me which direction he went?"

"One more cookie."

"Unbelievable."

I set a five dollar bill on the counter and he jerked his thumb left. I grabbed my three twenty-five dollar peanut-butter cookies, and left.

CHAPTER TWENTY-FIVE

I walked west along Rowena in the hot sun, squinting through my motorcycle cop sunglasses, eyes pealed for a bum and his dog.

If I were a bum with a freshly procured bottle of the good stuff, where would I take it? Well, I would want to drink it ASAP, of course, especially if I was an alcoholic. Also, I would want my privacy, especially if I was drinking the good stuff. No passing the bottle around a tent city.

So it would have to be close, and it would have to be cool, and it would have to be away from the cops. I paused, scanning the area. To the north was a high school. To the south were nicer two-story homes. Neither direction was bum friendly.

I continued west. I was close, I knew it. Somewhere nearby a bum was drinking. Safe from prying eyes. I turned left down an alley, between an auto body shop and a dry cleaners and came to a parking lot which was mostly empty of cars, and definitely empty of bums. I retreated back to the sidewalk, stopped, scanned the street again, wiped sweat from my brow...and saw something promising.

At the far end of the street was a construction site, a half-finished shopping center, in fact. The place was empty and lifeless, surrounded by a pathetic-looking chain link fence that was doing more leaning than standing.

Very bum friendly.

An ounce or two of sweat later, I was there at the site, moving along the lean-to fence until I found a gap big enough for a guy my size to squeeze through. Once inside, I stepped over a loose smattering of two-by-fours, deftly avoided a jutting carpenter's nail, and headed over to the partially finished building.

Here, I pulled out my shiny new toy. Dog whistles are a bit of a mystery to man. Or, at least, a mystery to *this* man. You blow the damn thing, nothing comes out but a lot of hot air, and yet dogs perk right up. Makes you wonder what else they're hearing that we can't.

Anyway, with the sun high above and a small breeze working its way over the exposed dirt and rock of the construction site, I lifted the narrow whistle to my lips and blew as hard as I could into it.

And heard nothing, of course, but before I was done blowing the reaction was immediate. Dogs from seemingly everywhere were barking at once. And furiously.

And through the cacophony of barks, which ranged from deep-throated woofs to high-pitched yipes, one particular bark stood out above the rest. It was deep and low and deliberate, and not nearly as energetic as some of the others. It was the bark of an old dog, and it was coming from directly inside the partially-finished shopping center next to me.

* * *

The building was framed, and some of the drywall was in place. I ducked under a low-hanging crossbeam and stepped into the cool shadows of the unfinished structure. The smell of sawdust was heavy in the air, along with something else. Urine.

It was also nearly pitch black. Damn. I had thought of the dog whistle, but I had missed the boat on a flashlight. Double damn. Still, who knew I would be crawling through a half-completed construction site?

Always come prepared, King.

As I made a mental note to buy a little flashlight to attach to my keyring, I waited for my eyes to adjust to the gloom, aided by the beams of sunlight slanting in through the many cracks and fissures in the incomplete structure. My own personal laser light show. Dust motes drifted in and out of the rays of light. In here, bustling L.A. seemed like a million miles away, or to have never existed. I was in a strange world of slanting light, crossbeams and unfinished cement slabs, with nothing to fill the heavy silence except my own labored breathing. Hell of a place to drink alone, if alone was your intent.

Finally my eyes adjusted—although *adjusted* might have been a bit too optimistic. *Less blind* was a little closer to the truth.

Anyway, I blew the whistle again, and again the nearby dogs barked excitedly, although not as many and not as vehemently. Except for one. Indeed, it barked deafeningly, and with a lot more energy than before, and would have raised the roof had there been a roof to raise. And it came from deeper within the structure.

Deeper was not necessarily better. Deeper meant darker.

Great.

I moved cautiously through the increasingly deepening shadows, and the further I went, the more the dog barked. As I guided myself carefully over the debris-strewn floor by running my hand along the exposed wooden wall frames, I worried about splinters and nails and being mauled by a really big dog with really big teeth.

Lots of worrying going on here.

I turned a corner and there, sitting in a splash of sunlight on a patch of dirt-covered cement, was a man and his dog. The man sported a dirty blond ponytail, and the dog sported a lot of teeth and black gums and raised hackles. The man was currently turning his head this way and that, trying to get a look at me coming out of the shadows.

"You a friend?" he asked.

"Yes."

He nodded, patted his dog, who immediately calmed down, although it still growled intermittently. "Not sure what got into him. He never acts like this."

I decided not to mention the dog whistle. "Maybe he doesn't like old men."

"Naw, Dusty likes everyone, unless you mean to do me harm."

"I'm just here to ask you some questions," I said.

"You with the police?"

"Nope."

He grinned and patted the cement slab next to him. "Then pull up a chair, my friend, and let's have a drink."

CHAPTER TWENTY-SIX

There was, of course, no chair to pull up.

My eyes continued adjusting. We were in a corner space that I imagined would someday be the waiting room to a dentist's office, complete with outdated magazines, uncomfortable furnishings and broken toys for kids who ate way too much sugar.

"Hot out today," I said.

"But cool in here," he said.

"And dark."

He grinned. He seemed to like the dark part the best, and I didn't blame him. A bum could disappear in here; at least, until construction started again. Milton looked bad, even for a bum. His sunken cheeks were dark hollows and his long blond hair was thinning badly. In fact, it appeared to be falling out in clumps. Yeah, maybe he was dying. He drank some more booze. The sound of it sloshing around inside the bottle was amplified inside this small, contained space.

"My name's Aaron," I said.

"Milton," he said, and took another long pull on his whiskey. "My name's Milton and I'm dying."

"I'm sorry."

"Sorry that I'm dying, or sorry that my name's Milton?" He laughed and slapped his knee hard and a cloud dust exploded off it, drifting up in the slanting rays of sunlight.

"Milton's a fine name," I said, and stepped closer. As I did so, Dusty growled a little, but not very energetically. I took out a cookie and unwrapped it. Dusty quit growling and wagged his tail instead. Food talks.

"May I?" I asked Milton.

"Knock yourself out, man."

Dusty the Mutt had a lot of golden retriever in him. He also needed a bath, and no doubt all of his shots. I broke off a piece of the cookie and tossed it over to him, and Dusty promptly snatched it clean out of the air, even in the near darkness. He threw back his head like a whooping crane and swallowed the piece of cookie without so much as tasting it. For all he knew I could have tossed him my watch. Anyway, Dusty's alert, glowing eyes were back on me again, ready for some more cookie, or anything else I might throw at him. I decided to keep my watch.

"You need some money?" Milton asked suddenly, reaching into a pocket hidden within the many layers of his clothing. Amazingly, he pulled out a small wad of cash, counted out a few bills for me, and held them out. "We could all use a little extra money, friend. I had a good day today. Here, have some of it. Buy yourself something to eat."

I was oddly touched. "I'm okay, Milton, but thank you."

He held out the bills a few moments longer, then shrugged and absently shoved them back somewhere inside his voluminous clothing. I was fairly certain the wad never made it back into the same pocket. Milton had already drank half his bottle. If he wasn't drunk now, he would be soon. If I wanted any answers, I'd better get them now.

"Have you ever shopped at Trader Joe's, Milton?" I asked.

He didn't answer at first. Instead, he took a long pull from the bottle, then held it out to me when he was finished. Tempted as I was, I declined. He shrugged and set it down on the concrete next to him. The sound of whiskey splashing back and forth echoed hollowly, sounding bigger than it really was in this small, unfinished room. Milton, I was certain, was getting drunker by the minute. I broke off another piece of cookie and tossed it over to Dusty. He missed it this time, but promptly plucked it off the ground.

"Milton, you ever shop at Trader's Joe's?" I asked again.

"Where?"

"Trader Joe's," I said patiently.

"I'm dying," he said.

"I'm sorry to hear that."

"I have cancer. I can feel it eating away right here." He touched underneath his left arm and my first thought was pancreatic cancer, but then again, what did I know?

"I'll get you help," I said.

"I don't want help," said Milton. "I want to die."

Milton dropped his head forward and I saw clearly where his hair was falling out. I also saw scabs and various wounds. He had been beat up recently. Or had fallen. Or had contracted some disease or another. There was a time in my life when I could not do this, that I *would not* do this. Conversing with a bum in a forgotten construction site, exposed to germs and craziness and the unknown. But I was a different man back then. Different needs, different desires, different phobias. Now my desire was to do my job and to do it well—and to find Miranda and bring her back safely to her mother. Whatever it took, even if it meant being here now, in a forgotten construction site with a forgotten man, and a dog whose appetite would not be ignored.

I tossed him another chunk of cookie.

Milton and I were silent. He kept holding his side, wincing. The smell of urine was stronger in here. I suspected the stench was coming from Milton himself.

"Milton," I said, then repeated his name louder before I got his attention. "Milton, when were you last in Trader Joe's?"

He started nodding. "When I saw the girl."

I sucked in some air that was also suffused with the smell of sawdust and dog breath. "Who was the girl?" I asked.

"Prettiest thing I ever did see. Made me want to live again."

"The girl's missing, Milton. Something bad happened to her. Something very bad."

Milton began shaking his head, and he kept on shaking it, and in the dim light of the unfinished room, I could see the urgency in his rheumy eyes. Dusty moved closer to him, nuzzling him.

"I didn't do anything to her," he said.

"Did you see what happened to her, Milton?"

He started clawing his neck. Maybe his cancer was there, too, eating away at his throat. "I didn't hurt her. She was too beautiful to hurt. I just wanted to look at her."

"So you followed her around the store?"

He nodded. "You woulda, too, my friend. So pretty. Long brown hair." He was getting drunker. Words slurring. I was losing him.

He started weeping, hard, and the moment he did, as if on cue, Dusty began howling with him, throwing back his head like a hound dog. I'm partial to hound dogs.

"I'm dying," he said again, blubbering, his words barely discernible.

"I'm sorry, Milton."

"I wanted to touch her so bad."

"Did you touch her?"

He shook his head once and cried even harder, and Dusty was howling and periodically licking his dirty tears. Jesus.

"Did you follow her outside, Milton?" He didn't hear me. I repeated the question.

"Yeah," he finally said.

My heart was hammering now. The empty room was suddenly stifling. I swallowed hard and wished I had brought a bottle of water. Hell, even his back-washed whiskey was looking pretty damn good about now.

"What happened outside?" I said, pushing, keeping him focused.

He stopped crying on a dime and looked off to his side, eyes glazed and wet and distant. "He took her."

With his sudden silence, Dusty fell quiet as well, looking from me to him, as if for an explanation to what had just happened. I had none to give.

"Who took her, Milton?"

When he spoke again, he did so hollowly, his voice barely discernible. "A man. In a van." He laughed, or cried, at his own rhyme.

"What color was the van?"

"White."

"Who was driving the van, Milton?"

"A man," he said again. "Ugly as sin. Holes in his face."

"Holes?" I said. "Pock marks?"

"Yeah, those."

"Did she fight him?" I asked. "Did he force her into the van?"

"I don't know, man. When I came around the corner she was already in."

"Did she look scared, Milton?"

He shook his shaggy head. "I don't know, man. I don't know."

I asked him more questions—all the questions I could think of—but Milton clearly had no clue where she was taken to, or why she had gotten in the van, or who the man was. And as he lapsed into an impenetrable, drunken stupor, I set the remaining cookies next to him, patted Dusty on the head, and left.

"I'm dying," he said behind me.

"I'm sorry," I said, and kept walking.

CHAPTER TWENTY-SEVEN

The L.A. Philharmonic is in downtown Los Angeles, and is located in the now famous Walt Disney Concert Hall. The Disney Hall, itself a modern-day marvel of neo-expressionistic architecture, which basically means *weird*, has been featured in everything from *Iron Man* to the *Simpsons* and from commercials to popular podcasts. The structure, which looks a bit like an ocean wave frozen in time and space, boasts laser-fitted stainless steel panels and sweeping, jutting walls that defy gravity and boggle the mind. Well, at least boggle *my* mind.

Anyway, I was heading over to it now for a concert, and I was running late, having lost all track of time while reading through Miranda's police file for the hundredth time, looking for anything that stood out, anything the police might have missed. So far, nothing stood out. At least not yet. Oh, and the freak summer rainstorm didn't help matters much. Five minutes of pouring rain that included two loud thunderclaps. Scared the shit out of my cat. Dogs in the neighborhood, spooked, had immediately started barking. As if on cue, the short downpour immediately bottled-necked Figueroa Avenue, proving once again that L.A. drivers have no clue how to drive in the rain.

Frustrated and ornery, I pulled into the adjoining parking lot, shelled out $9 that I would never see again, and hurried up a steep side street. Steep, that is, to these old knees.

As you might imagine, the evening was cool and damp. I was dressed in jeans and a flannel, not the attire of choice for the L.A. Philharmonic elite, but I happened to know its president, and I happened to know that the word was out that the L.A. Phil was actually encouraging casual attire to attract a wider audience.

Well, I was more than happy to oblige. I spent half my life in monkey suits. These days, flannel suited me just fine. Must be the country boy in me.

And there, standing near the glass entrance, dressed sharply in a wool coat with a fur collar, was my friend. A female friend. Her name was Grace, and she was also the aforementioned president of the L.A. Philharmonic, which means she courted the rich and famous for a living. Which means free tickets for me. She was young and in her early forties, blond and cute. She was also married to an ex-football player, and she thought of me, I think, as the grandfatherly type. I could handle that. I was indeed, after all, a grandpa. Anyway, I had helped her find her runaway son a few years back and ever since then I've been getting free tickets to the Phil. Admittedly, I usually *passed* on the free tickets, as the uppity scene just wasn't my style these days.

Also, chamber music blows hard. Granted, I'm a fan of most music, and I do enjoy Bach and Mozart whenever I'm trapped in an elevator. But sitting through an entire concert of the stuff is truly a question of how fast will I hit the seat in front of me, snoring.

Spotting me, Grace stepped away from a small gathering of people, gave me a big hug, and a not-so-big peck on the cheek.

"You're late," she said, straightening the shoulders of my flannel and brushing lint off my shoulders. I was unaware of the lint. Grace was also neat freak. Me, not so much.

"And your point?" I asked.

"I suppose, if you had been early, that would have been the bigger news."

"Exactly."

She gave me my ticket and led the way inside. Grace seemed to know everyone. She stopped often, shook many hands, hugged those who were hug-worthy, and, in general, looked like she ran the joint, which she happened to do.

"So why tonight of all nights?" she asked as we boarded the escalator up. "You've turned down all my other invitations."

"I dig Indian folk music."

"Bullshit," she said.

"Well, someone has to."

She laughed. "Well, Raffi is, in fact, world-famous."

"With a name like that, how could he not be?"

She squeezed my arm, nearly snuggling against me. Flannel has that effect on women. She smelled of good perfume. Her skin was flawless. Her features were small and sharp, her eyes large and round and very blue.

"Not to mention, Raffi and I share the same birthday," I added.

"So it was a sign," she said. "You are big on signs."

"Signs are important," I said. "They mean something. It's sort of like the universe speaking to you."

"Or God," she said.

I nodded. "Or God."

We got off the escalator. She hurried me along a short tunnel where we joined a small throng of theater-goers. An usher was checking tickets, and was about to check ours when he looked up at Grace, the boss of bosses. He swallowed hard, smiled, and stepped aside, letting us through.

"Hey, he didn't check my stub," I said.

Grace squeezed my hand and pulled me along through an archway and into grand concert hall. She led the way up a few rows and slid into what I knew were the management seats. Not quite in the middle, but close enough. People paid damned good money for the middle seats, after all.

Oh, and grand it was. Holy shit. The main hall was massive and elegant, and the dichotomy between the cold metallic exterior and the soft woods of the interior, with its curved balconies and railings, couldn't have been more striking. And since the L.A. Phil was built with Disney money, that meant the place was also cursed to look cartoonish. Example: the suspended wooden ceiling was supposed to be a stylized ship's hull, except that it looked more like something Jack Sparrow would have captained in The Pirates of the Caribbean. And the elegant organ behind the stage, although a magnificent piece of modern art with its soaring brass pipes, still looked like the world's biggest bag of French fries. Intentional or not, subliminal or not, I was now jonesing for some McDonald's.

"The real question," said Grace, once we were settled, "is how you *interpret* the signs."

"Are we still on this?" I asked.

"Yes. Now, you must have been troubled with something, Aaron, or perhaps you were faced with a decision. And, in the middle of all this indecision, here appears a rather famous Indian sitarist who shares your exact birthday. So here you are, hoping that God will continue to speak to you, continue to guide your way. And all you have to do is follow the signs."

"Are you quite done?" I asked.

"But am I right?"

"Maybe."

"What are you struggling with, Aaron King?" she asked me. She tightened her grip around my arm. She was always very touchy-feely.

I opened my mouth to speak but a small man sporting a long gray ponytail approached Grace, hugged her tightly, chatted a bit and then left again. She didn't bother to introduce me, nor did he seem particularly interested in me, anyway.

"Go on," she said. "What are you struggling with?"

I took a deep breath. Held it. Took another one. Held it. Plunged forward. "I'm thinking about getting back into music," I said.

"Ah," she said, smiling smugly. "Yes, of course, you were a singer back in the day. I think you mentioned that once or twice when you were shit-faced drunk. And when I asked you about it later, you were not pleased that I knew."

"Yeah, well, my singing was a long time ago."

"And, on the very day you were struggling with that decision, you get my email invitation from me about this concert."

"Everyone hates a know-it-all," I said.

"And, being the observant investigator that you are, you happened to see the similarities in birthdays, and considered it a sign from God," she said. "And now here you are."

"You talk a lot," I said. "Even for a broad."

She smiled some more at me. "So what did you mostly sing back in the day? Rock, country?"

"Indian folk," I said.

She looked at me some more. "You don't want to talk about it, do you?"

"No, not yet."

A true friend, she let it drop and gave me another forearm squeeze. I like squeezes.

As the house lights went down, the announcer politely asked in his pleasantly rich baritone to please refrain from taking any pictures and to please turn off all cell phones. And because he asked so nicely, I turned mine off and somehow refrained from taking any pictures, tempted as I was.

***

And by the end of the evening, after two hours of listening to traditional Indian folk music, I came to a decision about my own music.

Lord help me, I came to a decision.

CHAPTER TWENTY-EIGHT

The frames Dr. Vivian's glasses were wider than her head, making her narrow face even more narrow. I liked her narrow face. I liked her big glasses. I liked her, in fact, a lot.

"I find you very attractive," I said. We were halfway through my latest session, and I was finding her particularly distracting today, especially her big blue eyes.

"Isn't that a little off-topic?" she said. As she spoke, she didn't move a muscle. If my compliment surprised her, made her feel good, creeped her out, etc., you wouldn't know it by looking at her.

"Your beauty is never off-topic."

"Charming, Mr. King. But my beauty, or alleged beauty, is not the issue here," she said. "Besides, you don't find me attractive, not really."

"I don't?"

"No, you don't."

I chewed on that. Light from her lamp, which sat at the far corner of her desk, was casting angular shadows across her angular face. Angular or not, I was certain I found her beautiful. I said as much.

"It's called *transference*," she said.

"Transference?"

"It's when the patient develops strong feelings for his therapist."

"This has happened to you before?" I asked.

"Often."

"I see," I said. "And it's not because you're pretty."

She tilted her head. As she did so, her oversized glasses caught a lot of the lamplight and reflected it back at me tenfold, nearly blinding me. I exaggerate, of course, for emphasis.

She said, "On the streets, Mr. King—that is, in the real world—you wouldn't look at me twice."

"I wouldn't?"

"No. Especially not you, one who has had his fair share of the most beautiful women in the world."

"And you are not one of them?" I asked.

"Most certainly not," she said.

"Am I permitted to disagree?"

She looked at me steadily, unmovingly. If she were breathing, I couldn't tell. "Mr. King, you see a female sitting across from you, patiently listening to you, helping you, working with you, completely invested in you, viewing you without judgment or agenda. I represent all the people in your life who should love you but don't."

I took a deep breath. "You're not helping."

She sat back. "Mr. King, just know that I'm not your type and will *never* be your type, and you are far too old for me, so just get it out of your head."

"Ouch."

"Tough love," she said.

"Ah," I said. "So you do love me, then?"

Despite herself, she grinned, and some of the lamplight caught her tiny front teeth. "Let's get back to the business at hand, Mr. King."

"So we're changing the subject."

"Yes, we are," she said.

"Fine," I said. "But don't you have some questions for me?"

"What do you mean?"

"You just discovered a few days ago that your patient really is Elvis Presley, and you haven't asked me a single thing."

"Because we're not here for me," she said.

"You have a lot of will power," I said.

"Mr. King, as remarkable as your story is, as interesting as you might be, as storied as your life was and is, I still have a job to do. You pay me to help you—not act like a star-struck teenager."

"Are you star struck?"

She looked me square in the eye, which was appropriate, since the frames of her glasses were mostly square. "Mr. King, I see you as a very troubled man. My job is to help you through your troubles."

"Good luck," I said.

"No," she said, "Good luck to you, sir."

"So I'm not in love with you?" I asked again.

"No, I'm sorry."

"Maybe a little?"

"I seriously doubt it."

"Ah, hell."

CHAPTER TWENTY-NINE

I was at a donut shop on Glendale Avenue with the good Detective Colbert. It was early in the morning and the sun was just out, and so were many of the bums, many of whom were actively panhandling the local intersections.

"Let me get this straight," said Colbert. "The bum sees her in a van?"

"Yes."

"The bum's a credible witness?"

"He's a drunk and he's dying. His words."

"But you believe him."

"I think so, yes."

"So the bum follows the girl around the store and then out into the parking lot, where some guy in a van picks her up."

"That about sums it up," I said.

"Being driven by a menacing-looking character," Colbert said.

"With pock marks."

"Pock marks are menacing," Colbert said.

"That's an unfortunate stereotype," I said.

The donut shop was surprisingly packed. Across the street, through the big glass window, on a sidewalk in front of the Vons grocery store, was a homeless tent city, comprised of a dozen or so shopping carts filled to the brim with Lord knows what, covered with cardboard and blankets. Actually, the structure seemed fairly solid. Hell, so solid it was almost incorrect to call those within *homeless*. One way or another, that was certainly a home, complete with rooms and hallways. The ultimate kid's fort.

"I assume our friend didn't take down the license plate," said Colbert.

"No."

"Did he catch the color of the van?"

"White."

"Make and model?"

I shook my head. "Only that it didn't have any windows."

"A cargo van?"

"Be my guess."

"Great," said Detective Colbert, "I'll tell my men to be on the lookout for a white, windowless van driven by a sinister, pock-marked male, who may or may not have our damsel in distress held hostage in the back."

"Don't forget she appears to have gone willingly."

He chewed on that. "So she knows the guy."

"Be my guess."

"So she agrees to go with him wherever he asks her to go, and gets in the van, groceries and all."

"Must have been pretty important," I said. "For her to get in the van and leave her car."

He nodded.

I was working on a plain cake donut; Colbert was eating a ham and cheese croissant. I was of the opinion that if you went into a donut shop, you ate donuts, not croissants. We were both drinking non-fat milk.

"How come you're eating a plain donut?" he asked me.

"Watching my weight."

"Why?" he asked.

"I'm auditioning today at the Pussycat."

"For what?"

"A singer."

"A singing detective?" He grinned at his own joke. "You any good?"

"We'll see," I said.

I finished my donut and sipped the non-fat milk from the carton. I had completely butchered the carton while opening it, and I was now drinking from a tattered hole. Colbert seemed to be enjoying his croissant. As he spoke to me, his eyes scanned the crowd inside the donut shop. That was a cop thing, aware of your surroundings at all times. I was aware, too, but I just didn't care as much.

"How do we know Milton the Bum didn't do her," said Colbert. "And bury her body at this construction site?"

"We don't," I said.

"But you don't think so."

"I don't think so," I said.

"Your instincts as good as they say?" he asked.

"Sometimes better," I said.

"Okay," he said, "I'll tell my guys to keep looking for a mysterious white van, lot of good it'll do. You still working the case?"

"Yes."

"Good," he said, and stood. "I can use you. You're doing good work. What's your next step?"

"No idea," I said.

"Join the club."

CHAPTER THIRTY

I was driving west along Hollywood Blvd. The gray skies from days past were long gone, to be replaced by something hot and mean and shining down from above. Since the Cadillac's air conditioner had broken sometime during the Carter administration, I was driving with the windows down; hell, in this heat, I would have driven with the doors off, too, if I could.

The wind whipped my dyed hair, my shades were on, and I looked about as cool as cool gets. Maybe even cooler.

I knew Hollywood, and I knew it well, which is why I chose to finish out my days here. After all, I had made many movies here, with many fond memories. Bitter memories, as well, but fond nonetheless. Also, with all the whackos, I thought for sure I could disappear in Los Angeles, and for the most part I have.

I drove with the radio on and my elbow out the window. I preferred the golden oldies of the fifties and sixties. Go figure. At the moment my radio was tuned into K-Earth, and Chuck Berry was doing his groovy thing.

As I drove, I kept beat to the song by slapping the hot sheet metal of the door. I even sang a little, although I had long ago conditioned myself to *stop* singing, even when alone.

And as I sang, I discovered my upper lip curling at the corner. Okay, that had to *definitely* stop.

I passed Grauman's Chinese Theatre, and all the freaks were out. And so were the cartoon characters and impersonators. Spider-man was posing with an older Asian couple. The couple looked about as happy as could be. A Marilyn impersonator was blowing a passing car a kiss, and then she blew me a kiss, too. I winked at her. She winked back. It was a damn good impersonation.

And there, with his arms around an attractive young couple, mugging for the camera, was an Elvis impersonator. He was fat, and his thick sideburns were far too prominent. He was wearing aviator shades and my white rhinestone jumpsuit from the seventies.

Jesus, what the hell was I thinking back then?

I passed Grauman's and made a right and headed up the Sunset Strip. Now Johnny Cash was on the radio, and I had nothing but fond memories of the man and his wife, June.

Still early in the day, traffic on the strip was relatively light, although that would change with the onset of night. I passed the Whiskey A-Go-Go, the Comedy Club, the Rainbow Room, and there, situated between an adult bookshop and a Chinese take-out place, was the Pussycat, owned by one of the original members of the Stray Cats.

The Pussycat Theater, which catered to a thirty-five and older crowd, was having auditions today for a new lounge singer. *Elvis Presley, lounge singer extraordinaire.*

I parked the Cadillac along a side street, turned the engine off, and sat in the driver's seat for a few minutes, sweating and thinking. I asked myself again if I wanted to do this. If I really, truly wanted to do this.

I was pretty sure I did. Actually, I was damn sure. In fact, sitting here in my hot car, surrounded by beautiful homes and the world-famous clubs of the Sunset Strip, I was having a hard time remembering why I wanted out in the first place.

A decision I had made a long, long time ago.

I drummed my fingers on the hot steering wheel, which was growing hotter by the minute. Sweat beaded my brow. I used to get so damn hot on stage, sweat pouring from my body. But I loved the stage. I worked hard to entertain. No one could ever take that from me.

Yes, I very much wanted to sing again, but wasn't the risk of getting caught too great?

One problem was that my singing voice is fairly distinctive. Perhaps *too* distinctive. But wouldn't it have changed over time? My speaking voice had certainly changed over time into something far more rumbling and grittier.

Cars whipped past me, followed by a lot of hot billowing wind and spraying bits of sand and debris. Someone opened the door to the Pussycat across the street and live music thundered out, which made sense since they were in the middle of auditions.

Perhaps if I stayed away from my own songs, and sang something very *un*Elvis, and, for the love of all that which is holy, didn't curl my upper lip, well, I might just get away with this.

And if you don't?

I guess I'll just cross that bridge when I get there.

That's a helluva bridge.

I continued drumming my fingers. Sweat continued rolling from my brow. I closed my eyes and saw the crowd and tears and smiles. Taking a deep breath, I opened the door and slid off the hot leather seat, and then headed across the street to the Pussycat.

I had an audition. *Elvis* had an audition.

Go figure.

CHAPTER THIRTY-ONE

The nightclub was small and gloomy. A young man was currently on stage, singing loudly in front of a group of people. His voice, at least to my ears, was unpleasantly loud.

I headed straight to the bar and ordered a Newcastle on tap. The young bartender nodded, poured me one, set it in front of me. I immediately knocked most of it back. The bartender watched me, raising his eyebrows. I was damned thirsty; not to mention I needed to be liquored-up asap.

The bartender leaned a hip on the counter and went back to watching the auditions. So did I. The first singer, who had pitch problems, mercifully finished and was promptly thanked. He exited the stage as another singer walked on. I couldn't help but notice he was also in his forties.

You're going to be the oldest one.

I drank more. Standing in a pool of yellow light, this next singer sang something by Frank Sinatra. Or maybe Tony Bennett. Hell, I couldn't remember. I was finding it hard to concentrate. To breathe.

Huddled together on the dance floor, scribbling on clipboards, were a half dozen people. A tall man wearing blue shades wasn't scribbling. Instead, he was standing there with his arms crossed and looking formidable.

"Okay," he said, cutting off the singer in mid-croon. "Thank you, we've heard enough. We'll give you a call."

The man in the blue shades didn't sound like he would ever be giving him a call. It was a brush-off, a polite goodbye. And the singer wasn't that bad, either. Granted, he wasn't great, but he was certainly good enough to warrant finishing the song.

Suddenly, I was losing my nerve. I downed my beer, ordered another, drank it right there in front of the bartender, who was grinning at me.

"You must be here for the audition?" he said.

"How can you tell?"

He grinned some more. "Nervous?"

"As hell."

He laughed. "Bill can be a real asshole," he said, "but don't let him get to you. If you can sing, he'll be your best friend."

"Good to know. He the one with the cool blue shades?"

"Yeah, that's him, but I don't know about cool. You can sing, right?"

"We'll find out."

I sat through three more auditions, all male. Most had very pleasant voices. All were clearly professionals and all were about thirty years younger than yours truly.

"You don't think I'm too old, do you?" I asked the bartender.

He sized me up. The kid was handsome, and that grin of his probably had gotten him everything he wanted in life and more. I knew the feeling well.

"Naw, but to be safe, knock a few years off your age. No harm, no foul, right? Everyone does it. Remember that it's all about the singing. Oh, and the performing."

"Performing?"

"You know…" He jerked his hips a little. "Like Elvis. Bill loves Elvis."

Oh, shit.

I nearly ordered another beer, but refrained. I performed better sober. As it stood now, I was already a little buzzed.

When the last singer stepped off the stage, Bill the Manager flipped up his cool blue shades and looked around. His slicked-back hair reflected some of the overhead lights.

"That it?" he asked no one in particular. He didn't sound happy.

I said nothing and stayed rooted to the stool, my heart somewhere in my throat. I tried to give myself some positive self-talk, but my thoughts were scrambled and incoherent and I only knew one thing: *fear*. I couldn't get myself to move. My chance was slipping away....

"Okay, then—" Bill began, but never finished.

Why? Because the good-looking kid behind the bar suddenly leaned across said bar and shouted loudly: "Hey, Bill. We've got another one back here."

I didn't know whether to hug the kid or run.

"Then get the fuck out here," said Bill the Manager, flipping his shades back down. "Haven't got all fucking day."

Great, you've already pissed him off.

I downed the last of my beer, jumped off the stool, and promptly ran headlong into another stool. It went flying—and I nearly went flying, too. Luckily, I fell over onto a table. Yeah, luckily. Someone laughed. I heard Bill mumble "Jesus Christ", and all I wanted to do was run for the door and get the hell out of Dodge. Or, in this case, the Pussycat.

But the bartender was there in an instant, taking my elbow, helping me to my feet, dusting me off. "It's okay, man," he said to me quietly. "Calm down. You'll be okay. I'm rooting for you."

I smiled at him weakly. He straightened my collar, winked, and guided me through the maze of chairs and stools. Buzzed, discombobulated, and now in pain, I found myself moving numbly forward toward the stage and lights.

The Pussycat, which was a fairly small nightclub, suddenly seemed expansive and endless, and the stage itself seemed to recede exponentially with each step I took.

Suddenly Bill materialized before me, looming, easily two inches taller than me. "Wait," he said. His eyes, though mostly hidden behind the aforementioned blue shades, appeared to be searching my face. "What's your name?"

"Aaron King," I said. My mouth felt dry, even though I had just pounded a few beers.

He continued standing directly in front of me. Those behind him ignored me completely, their heads huddled together, referring to a master list. Already they were scratching off names.

"How old are you?" he asked.

"Fifty, um, five."

Surprisingly, he grinned. "Sure you are. Can you sing?"

"We'll see."

"Fine. What will you be singing?"

"'Ring of Fire,'" I said.

"Johnny Cash."

"Yup," I said.

"I love 'Ring of Fire,'" he said.

"Then you're not so bad," I said, "after all."

He stared at me some more, then shook his head and chuckled and asked a young girl sitting at a piano if she knew the song, and she said, "Hell, yeah." She sounded offended.

His blue shades settled back on me. "You're on," he said. "Don't suck."

And with those encouraging words ringing in my ears, I stepped up onto the stage, the first real stage I had been on in nearly thirty years. The wood creaked with each footfall. Stages always creak; I love that about them. Soon I stood front and center, blinking hard into the lights.

There were six of them beneath me, huddled together on the dance floor, ready to pass judgment. Beyond the dance floor, in the murky depths of the bar area, the young bartender was leaning a hip against the counter, a towel slung over his shoulder, arms crossed, watching me. He caught my eye and nodded, smiling.

Calmness radiated from the kid, a sort of infectious tranquility. So I focused on him, focused on his grin. I needed support, I needed faith, and he was the only one presently giving it to me.

God bless him.

My heart pounded.

Too hard, too fast.

The stage was semicircular. It was rutted and scraped and stained from years of amps and speakers and drums being hauled across it, from boots scraping it, from beer bottles slamming down on it.

In front of me was a single microphone stand, glowing in the single spotlight. I stepped slowly up to it. Bill checked his watch.

I clicked my fingers in front of the microphone, an old habit. The sound was good. I looked over to the young pianist. She was looking at me from over her shoulder, waiting for my cue, eager to get this show on the road. I nodded.

The music started. A simple song, really, but nearly impossible to sing right. So many have tried and so many have failed. Johnny Cash, my one-time friend, was a tough act to follow. And I should know. I followed him often enough.

And as the music started, and as I gripped the microphone in front me and looked out across the empty tables and booths and focused on that single, handsome face smilingly encouragingly at me from behind the bar, as the first words of the song rolled smoothly and easily off my tongue, and as my hips moved instinctively to the music, something amazing happened.

I had come home, and it was as if I had never left.

CHAPTER THIRTY-TWO

The music stopped and I let my voice trail off. My snapping fingers dropped to my side, and my tapping foot slowed, then stopped. There were tears in my eyes and joy in my heart. Whether or not I got the gig, I didn't care. I needed to do this. Bad.

Somebody was clapping. It was my friend from across the room, the bartender. He stopped long enough to give me a thumbs-up sign, then clapped some more.

Bill the manager was staring at me, his mouth slightly open. Well, at least I think he was staring at me. Hard to tell with those stupid shades. I was still coming down from my high and so I continued standing there on stage, in the spotlight, soaking it all in.

Now this is a high I can get used to.

Bill started nodding and he kept on nodding as he made his way to the others. He joined the group and everyone seemed to be talking at once.

As they did so, I closed my eyes and relived the moment—and it had been a helluva moment. At least for me nowadays. And as I relived this moment, the other moments flood back, too. The bigger moments. The grander moments. The crowds. The churning sea of smiling faces. God, I used to put so many smiles on so many faces. I could bring joy to others with my voice. I had forgotten about that. There's value to bringing joy to others. Immense value.

Bill finally stepped away from the others and came over to me. He stood below me on the dance, pushed his sunglasses up onto his forehead. The upper bridge of his nose was pinched and red where the rubber stabilizers had sat for God knows how long.

"Fucking incredible," he said.

"Thank you," I said. *Thank you. Thank you ver' much....*

"You're a little older than what we're looking for."

"I understand." My voice sounded distant and not quite my own. Only then did I notice the sweat pouring down my face.

"But we want to give you a shot. *I* want to give you a shot. Hell, I could listen to that—*to you*—all day and night. My God, King, you can sing."

"So I don't suck."

He smiled. "No, you don't. And you can move, too, for an old-timer."

"Go figure," I said.

"You'll have to show me that move sometime."

"Sure," I said. "After you pay me."

He laughed, and flicked down his shades again. Mr. Cool was back. "Can you be here Monday nights, starting next Monday at nine p.m.?"

"Yes, sir," I said.

"Good; see you then."

And as he turned away, I said, "And Bill?"

He looked back. "Yeah, King?"

"What's with the stupid blue sunglasses?"

He looked at me some more. I suspected he had once been a bouncer back in the day, before rising up to nightclub manager. "It's a good thing that you can sing lights out."

"Yeah, good thing."

He left and joined the others, and I walked slowly off the stage. Floating really. At the bar, the good-looking kid stepped around the counter, and slapped me heartily on the shoulder. I nearly fell over.

"You killed out there!" he said. I think he wanted to hug me but somehow refrained. Hell, I could have used a hug.

"Everyone gets lucky," I said.

"Then you must be the luckiest person on earth!"

"Yeah," I said. "I've been told that."

"Want a drink?"

"More than you know."

CHAPTER THIRTY-THREE

It was late, and the street was dark. I was sitting in my Cadillac with the engine off. Two houses down was a small house that wasn't so dark. In fact, the lights were on in just about every room. With my windows rolled down, I could just make some music issuing from the house.

It was 1:22 a.m.

I was flying high on Vicodin. I should have felt euphoric. Instead, as I watched the cheerfully-lit house in front of me, I felt numb and melancholy. In the big curtained front window, two figures would appear sometimes, dancing slowly, arm in arm, sometimes cheek to cheek.

Between my legs was a warm Sam Adams. I took a sip of it now and felt my melancholy deepen and take on a life of its own. A living, dark thing that dwelled inside me, like a parasite of the soul.

I had been following her for the past two weeks. Yes, she would hate me if she knew I had been following her. Well, what did you expect? I followed people for a living? What made her different?

You're supposed to trust her.

They usually ended up here, at this small house, followed by a lot of talking. And laughter. Then the music and dancing, their silhouetted faces sometimes pressed against each other in an intimate embrace.

I drank more warm beer. I wished I had brought more Vicodin. The pain in my heart was intense. Almost too intense.

Vicodin doesn't help heartache.

After being separated for nearly six months, Kelly and I had only recently gotten back together. I knew she had been dating while we were off-again, and I suspected this guy was a holdover from that.

Perhaps she didn't have the heart to let him go. Maybe she loved us both. Maybe she didn't give a fuck about my feelings. Or his feelings.

Fuck his feelings.

Kelly had said we had trust issues.

No kidding.

Now I watched as the man I both loathed and was curious about dipped Kelly romantically in front of the big window. I had, of course, looked into his background. I knew he lived modestly here in this small, suburban, three-bedroom home. No kids, never married. Twenty years my junior.

There was the rub.

Twenty years my junior.

You're an old man, King.

They stopped dancing and stood silhouetted in the window and kissed deeply. I took another swig from my warm beer.

Get a room.

Still kissing, still holding each other close, they fumbled away from the window and the living room lights went out. A few seconds later, a muted half-glow flickered from somewhere near the back of the house. Candlelight. The music was still playing, drifting across the quiet street.

I started my car and left, tossing the empty beer bottle onto my girlfriend's boyfriend's front lawn.

CHAPTER THIRTY-FOUR

I was in Dr. Vivian's office on an overcast morning. The window behind her was gray. The office, despite being cheerfully lit, felt gray. Perhaps my mood was gray, too.

"Is your twin single?" I asked.

"That's not an appropriate question, Mr. King."

"I shouldn't even be alive, so what the hell do I care about appropriateness?"

"Because you're not a buffoon."

"Is that a clinical term?"

Dr. Vivian smiled and shook her head. "Fine. She's happily married with four kids."

"And you?" I asked.

"That's a *very* inappropriate question, Mr. King."

"Just expressing my inner buffoonery."

She shook her head; she might have sighed, too. "No, Mr. King, I'm not married."

"Are you dating anyone?"

I noticed Dr. Vivian's cheekbones caught some of the desk lamp light. Her hair glowed softly. All of it framed against the gray, curtained window behind her. She pursed her lips, looking at me somewhat sternly.

"I know, I know," I said, "*highly* inappropriate."

"Thank you."

"Well?"

She suddenly laughed, and the unexpected, high-pitched sound of it surprised the hell out of me. "Any other patient," she said, "and I would have put an end to this line of questioning long ago."

"But I'm not any other patient?"

"No," she said. "You're not."

"And why is that?"

"Because you're Elvis-fucking-Presley."

"I haven't been him for thirty years."

"Fine," she said. "You *were* Elvis-fucking-Presley. That weighs heavily on my mind."

"I've forgotten what it's like to have his influence over other people."

"It's powerful," she said.

"Too powerful for you to resist?"

"I don't know," she said. "I'm doing things with you that I swore I would never do with patients. You're affecting my judgment."

"I don't want your judgment affected," I said, although I wasn't sure I meant it.

She was silent for a long moment. "I'm not sure that's possible now."

"Then perhaps we should move on with today's session," I said, winking.

"Hey," she said, "that's my line."

CHAPTER THIRTY-FIVE

"So, you're stumped," said Kelly.

We were walking along a semi-gravel trail through Griffith Park, which lies north of Los Feliz and Hollywood. The park is home to the L.A. Zoo and the Griffith Observatory, itself made infamous by one James Dean. I miss that little rebel.

"You could say that," I said.

We were holding hands, our fingers loosely interlaced. Kelly was dressed in tight black fuzzy sweats, a tight sweater and sneakers with gold trim. I was in workout pants and a tee shirt. My sneakers, surprisingly, had no gold trim. The day was warm, but not inordinately so. We traveled mostly through shadows along the heavily vegetated trail, thick with oaks and spruces. Squirrels dashed madly across the trail, up trees and through the chainlink fence that led off to the Los Feliz Golf Course.

"So you have a white van driven by an ugly guy with acne scars, as witnessed by a bum who was stalking the very same girl, the bum being witnessed by a box boy who was stalking the very same girl."

"Lots of stalking going on," I said.

"This girl, somehow, elicits this kind of behavior in men."

"She's a beautiful young lady," I asked.

"And she may not understand, or comprehend, her full effect on men."

"Meaning?"

"A simple glance, an innocent smile, an innocuous flip of her hair in the wrong direction at the wrong time could have the wrong guy panting and thinking very unclean thoughts."

"You make it seem like the males of our species have no control over themselves."

Kelly looked at me, raised her eyebrows. "Is that really a road you want to go down?"

"Fine," I said. "We have no control over ourselves."

"Look, all I'm saying is that most girls, especially pretty girls, learn at a young age to avoid eye contact, keep their face passive and non-expressive."

"Because to do otherwise—"

"Is to invite trouble," said Kelly.

"I seem to recall you smiling rather brilliantly at me when we first made eye contact."

"It's different when you think the guy is a cutie," said Kelly.

"You think I'm a cutie?"

"No," she said. "I think you're beautiful. In fact, I'm hard pressed to find a more beautiful man anywhere."

"Even for an old guy?"

"You've aged wonderfully, and you've always reminded me of someone, but I've never been able to put my finger on it."

"Brad Pitt?"

She shook her head, squeezed my hand.

"I don't know. Someone," she said.

"So why are we having such a hard time getting along?"

"Because beauty is only skin deep."

"We have other issues," I said.

"Attraction isn't one of them."

We were quiet some more as our sneakers crunched over loose gravel. Before us the road widened and curved past the northern end of the golf course.

"I do want to keep seeing you, Aaron," she said.

"Good."

"But I want to see other people, too."

I took in some air. A lot of air. We kept walking. Now the trees opened up and the sun beat down. I was dripping sweat.

"I know," I said.

"You know what?"

"You've been seeing someone for quite some time."

She released my hand. "How do you know that, Aaron?"

"I'm a private investigator. Put it together."

"You were following me?"

"It's what I do."

"How long have you known?"

"Since the first week we tried doing this again. You sent him an email from the computer at my house. You left your email up."

"And you read my email."

"It's what I do."

"Bullshit," she said. "Snooping on your girlfriend's private email is not what you do. You follow cheating husbands and wives, you find runaways and missing teens, but you don't have a right to read my email."

"No, I didn't."

"Well, aren't you going to apologize?"

"No."

"You don't think you did anything wrong?"

"I didn't say that. I'm just not going to apologize."

"Why not?"

I said nothing.

"Oh, no," she said. "You're not going to clam up on me now. Don't pull that shit on me again."

"Hey, this was supposed to be a peaceful walk," I said.

"That's out the window. Why won't you apologize?"

"Because you were cheating, Kelly. Look at the bigger picture. You're doing what you do best and diverting the attention away from the bigger issue. We both know that I'm a private eye, we both know that I make a living snooping into other people's lives—yes, even the lives of my girlfriends. You made a deliberate act to continue seeing another man, even while we were trying to mend our relationship."

"Why didn't you say something?"

"I was waiting to see what would happen."

We rounded the final curve of the golf course and were now headed toward the Greek Theater. In silence, we moved past the theater and adjacent housing track filled with opulent homes.

"I'm sorry I didn't tell you about him," she said after a while.

"Thank you," I said.

"I was waiting to see where things were going with us."

"So where are things going with us?" I asked.

"I love you, you big lug, but you're so closed, so secretive. It's hard for me to get around that."

"I understand."

"But, dammit, I want to still see you," she said. "But I also want to see other people, too."

"You mean you want to *continue* seeing other people," I said.

"Yes. To continue."

We walked in silence some more, then I said, "So we'll have one of those fancy, high-tech, open relationships everyone talks about?"

She laughed. "Yeah, something like that."

"And I can date other people, too?"

"That's how it works," she said, although I could hear the hesitancy in her voice.

"And you're not afraid of losing me?" I asked.

"I'm terrified," she said.

CHAPTER THIRTY-SIX

Euphoria. Pure, unadulterated euphoria.

An hour earlier I had taken my ninth Vicodin followed by a beer chaser, and now I was feeling high as a kite and pain free and at peace with the world around me.

Everyone should feel this good.

Maybe they do. Maybe I'm the one who's missing out.

I was in my living room. It was early afternoon and the sun was shining straight through my blinds and into my apartment. Earlier, the bright light had given me a headache.

But not anymore.

Vicodin gets rid of headaches. Vicodin gets rid of *all* aches. And on top of that, it makes you feel so damn good that even the bright sunlight is no longer a problem. Hell, *nothing* is a problem.

You're now well beyond the recommended daily dosage, Mr. King. I think it's official: you might just have a problem.

Sure I did, but I didn't care; at least not now.

Taking Vicodin with a beer chaser was a big no-no, as alcohol did something that increased something, but I didn't care. At least not now.

Don't try this at home, kids....

I felt so damn good and my head felt so damn clear, but I knew I had a serious fucking problem and I knew this problem was threatening to get out of control.

I'll deal with it later.

Always later, right King?

For now, my knees were no longer sore and my head was no longer hurting; my lower back felt damn good and even my jaw had quit throbbing, a jaw that had been hurting since my re-constructive plastic surgery thirty years ago.

Feeling good like I should.

I lay back on my sofa, rested my head on a throw pillow, and closed my eyes. My body felt wonderful. My body felt healthy. My body felt strong.

Everyone should feel this good....

CHAPTER THIRTY-SEVEN

It was later, and I was still feeling good as I read through Miranda's police file for the umpteenth time, focusing my attention this time around on Miranda's last boyfriends.

Jason Anderson, her most recent ex-boyfriend who now lived in New York, didn't have a clue what happened to Miranda. His story was fairly simple: Miranda had broken up with him a year or so ago after she had caught him cheating. He'd made several attempts to win her back but she wanted nothing more to do with him.

Good for her.

Police investigators had checked him out completely; he was clean. Besides, he had a rock-solid alibi at the time of her disappearance and the police had dropped him from the suspect list.

My instincts told me there was nothing there. I dropped him, too, the cheating bastard.

Generally, twenty-two-year-old girls didn't run away. Hell, at that age, it was called *moving*. But Miranda had lived a very easy and sheltered life with her mother. Miranda's mental and personal growth had no doubt been stunted by a few years.

Just a beautiful girl with no clue just how beautiful she really is.

The police had checked out all the hotels in Vegas but nothing had turned up under her name. They did the same for Reno and Laughlin and Tahoe. Nothing. They checked with current friends and old friends. Nothing. According to her friends, Miranda had had only one other significant boyfriend, a high school sweetheart named Flip

Barowski, now six or seven years removed. The detectives, perhaps considering Flip was too far removed, never bothered contacting him.

I got up from my chair. Oops, too fast. Instantly lightheaded, I guided myself over to my corner desk and sat down. I opened Miranda's personal case file and flipped back a dozen or so pages until I found the letter I had removed from her bureau drawer. The love letter.

I read it again.

Flip apparently had it bad for Miranda. Very bad. And in his letter he was apologizing for something again and again, but, unfortunately, he didn't say *why* he was apologizing. He ended the letter very succinctly: he threatened to end his own life if he could not have her.

Now that's love. Or infatuation.

Either way, I grabbed my car keys and headed out the door. I was really too buzzed to drive, but that never stopped me before.

Don't try this at home, kids.

CHAPTER THIRTY-EIGHT

I was on the road, buzzed and high, when Becky the pianist from the Pussycat called.

"Hey, good-looking," she said.

"Hey, pretty mama."

Oops. *Too Elvis.*

"Do you even know who this is?" she asked, giggling.

I pulled out onto Morton Ave and headed down through the hills of Echo Park. The reception here was fuzzy at best.

"No," I said, "unless it's Becky from the Pussycat."

"How did you know?"

"I'm good at voices."

"Well, I'm very impressed," she said.

I was driving by the shabbier homes of lower Echo Park. The day was sweltering. I turned right onto Glendale and picked up speed. My window was mostly up to hear better, my cell's earpiece shoved deep into my ear canal.

"So do you really think I'm good-looking?" I asked.

"I think you're beautiful," she said. "Especially your voice."

Becky sounded as if she were on something. Join the club. I think we were both feeling flirty and lonely and high.

"Even for an old geezer?" I asked.

She giggled. "You're only fifty-something, right?"

Close, but not quite.

"Old enough to be your father," I said.

"You can be my daddy anytime, sugar," she said, giggling again, and then she got to the point, which was probably for the best. "We need to rehearse sometime this week."

"Am I that bad?"

"No, you're that *good*. I think one rehearsal ought to do it. Can you come by the Cat this afternoon? Say three-thirty?"

I told her I would and we clicked off. I was now on Sunset Blvd. and heading west into the setting sun. I flipped down my shades.

Cool as cool gets.

* * *

The euphoria from the prescription drugs was wearing off.

And with its passing came the all-pervasive pain in my knees and back, and it came back with a vengeance.

I hate when that happens.

I need more Vicodin. Bad.

Ignoring the pain as best as I could, I parked in front of Dana's oversized house, ignored the faux dog, and knocked on her heavy front door.

A moment later, she appeared, and she didn't look good. Eyes bloodshot and vacant. Hair awry and forgotten. Dried tears crusting in the corner of her eyes and down her cheeks. She looked at me blankly for a moment or two, then turned and retreated back into her home. She left the door open and I followed her in, shutting it behind me. The house was dark and dead, shades drawn, lights off. Despite my lingering high, I felt miserable just being here.

As I followed her, I saw that my hands were shaking badly. I hadn't had the shakes in decades, not even with the drinking.

It's happening again.

King, you need help.

Ya think?

In the main living room, Dana fell into a wide, overstuffed chair, and reached immediately for a cut crystal tumbler that was filled with amber liquid. I was willing to bet the amber liquid wasn't lemonade.

She hadn't spoken, and I didn't bother asking her how she was doing. I knew how she was doing: *not good at all.*

"Your daughter didn't date much," I said simply.

She rolled her head my direction. "No."

"Why?"

"None of the guys were good enough, I guess."

"For you or her?" I asked.

"Both. I watched over her carefully, vigilantly. We weren't going to settle for just anyone."

"Her last boyfriend was a guy named Jason."

"Yes."

"No one since?" I asked.

"No one that I know of."

"Did she date anyone before Jason?"

"No."

"Not even casually?"

"I wouldn't allow it."

Hell, maybe Miranda *had* run away. I chewed my lip, a bad habit, and looked at the woman sitting across from me. She was obviously on some type of sedative to help deal with her daughter's disappearance.

"Did she date in high school?"

"Yes, one boy."

"What happened to him?"

"They broke up."

"Why?"

"Because they were just kids; it wasn't meant to last."

"Did you facilitate the break-up?"

"No. Actually, the boy played a trick on her."

I sat up a little straighter.

"A trick?" I said.

She turned her head slowly toward me again and blinked long and dramatically, and for the first time today she seemed to really look at me.

"Excuse me," she said, "but why the hell are you asking questions about my daughter's boyfriend from fucking high school?"

I opened my mouth to answer but she didn't let me answer, and suddenly, now given an outlet, all of her anger and frustration and fear was directed onto me.

"I demand to know what the fuck you've been up to, Mr. Aaron fucking King!"

Ah, yes. When a client asks for a full accounting—or, in this case, demands—by law I have to give them one. In this situation, I would have preferred to wait, but she was calling me out, so to speak, and so I caught her up to date on the investigation.

Dana did not know about the Trader Joe's employee, or the bum, or the van driven by the man with pockmarks, and when I was done she lost it. Just lost it.

Tears sprung fully formed from her eyes, spilling down over sharp cheekbones. She dropped the tumbler in her lap, spilling the booze everywhere. I was by her side instantly, plucking the glass up, and wrapping an arm around her shaking shoulders while she sobbed into my chest.

Aaron fucking King to the rescue.

When she was done, when she had gained some semblance of control over herself, I slipped off the chair's arm and sat on the ornate glass coffee table directly across from her. I took both her hands in mine. They were shaking nearly as bad as my own.

"I didn't think I had tears enough to cry," she said.

Tears enough to cry. Sounded like a sad, sad song.

Not everything is a song, King.

Oh, yeah?

"So she was kidnapped by some son-of-a-bitch in a van," she said.

I sucked in some air. "I think so, yes. The police are looking for the van now."

"But it could be anywhere, *she* could be anywhere, dead in the desert, tortured and raped and burned alive for all I know."

"We don't know that."

"But it's a very real possibility."

I didn't want to lie to her, and so I squeezed her hands and said nothing.

"Help me find her, King. Please. I'll give you anything you want. Please help me find my baby. Please, oh God, please…."

I patted her hand and made sympathetic noises, and after awhile I said, "Tell me about the boy in high school."

"But I don't understand—"

"Neither do I, but I have nothing else to go on, Dana. And since I don't have enough time or manpower to cruise the city streets looking for the white van, I'm going to do what I have been trained to do, which is to turn over every rock and stone until your daughter shows up."

"And one of those stones is her high school boyfriend?"

"Yes," I said. "Exactly. Now please tell me the trick he played on her, the reason she broke up with him."

"Her boyfriend was a twin."

I inhaled sharply. There it was again. *Twins.*

"Go on," I said.

"They were dating for nearly their entire senior year when the boy decided to do something stupid. Very, very stupid."

"What?"

She looked away. "He let his twin brother rape Miranda."

"I'm not sure I'm following—"

"The sons-of-bitches played a trick on her, King. One twin stepped out of the room—her boyfriend—and the other stepped in—his brother, dressed identically from head to foot, to fool her. Granted, it was late at night and everyone had been drinking, but Miranda knew something was wrong the moment he forced himself on her. She tried to stop him, but couldn't. I told him that if I ever saw him or his fucking perverted brother again, I would kill them both."

I didn't doubt it.

"Do you have a picture of Flip?" I asked.

"He's in her high school yearbook somewhere."

"Would you mind?"

She didn't, or at least not very much. She left the room and came back a few minutes later lugging a bright green high school yearbook. She sat next to me on the glass coffee table, flipped open the book. A moment later, she found the right page. Her partially painted fingernail, which was worried down to a mere nub, pointed to a handsome young man with a thick neck and spiky blond hair. His identical twin brother was next to him. Flip and Bryan Barowski. Both had fairly clear complexions.

Which meant neither matched the description of our pock-marked driver.

Strike one *and* two.

CHAPTER THIRTY-NINE

Clarke and I were at the Hollywood YMCA. He was doing bench presses on a shining new machine, and I was doing shoulder raises on an older machine that wasn't so shiny.

"They say that you get more definition if you use free weights," I said when we both finished our respective sets. "So why are we not using free weights?"

Clarke's face was still slightly purple with the strain of his recent pressing. A pulsating, lightning bolt-like vein slashed down across his forehead, Harry Potter-like. Clarke was tired of all my Harry Potter jokes. Unfortunately for him, I wasn't, since I was a closet Harry Potter fan.

"Because we're not thirty anymore," he said, "and we don't care about definition."

"We don't?"

Clarke leaned back and cranked out ten more reps. When finished, he sat forward again. Good thing, because the lightning bolt-like vein looked like it was about to burst.

"No," he said. "And if you say anything about the throbbing, lightning bolt-like vein on my forehead I'm going to go fucking ape-shit on you, King. Fucking ape-shit. I see you looking at it now."

I ignored him, or pretended to. "If we're not here for definition, Harry, then what the hell are we doing in the gym?"

"My name isn't fucking Harry, and we're here to prolong our lives."

"And why would we want to do that?"

"Because it's better than the alternative," he said. He looked over at me, sweat dripping from the tip of his nose. He shook his head and grinned. "You're a real asshole sometimes, you know."

"I know."

And he kept on looking at me. "Sitting here, in this light, you look exactly like him."

"That's because I *am* him, Clarke."

We were alone in the small weight room. Just around the corner next to us was the entrance to the women's locker room. Woohoo! Sometimes, when the door opened wide enough, you could catch a glimpse inside. And each time it did, Clarke and I automatically leaned a little to the side to get a better view. Just two harmless, although slightly perverted, old men. But, alas, it was the middle of the day and the Y was quiet, with only a handful of women coming and going.

"I know that," he said, "but with all the plastic surgery it's easy to forget...." his voice trailed off as he studied me some more. I hate being studied. "Upon first glance, you look nothing like him. You added a dimple to your chin and did something with your eyes and lips. Your disguise is perfect. You sound perfect. But sometimes, when you smile—"

"Let's drop it," I said, cutting in.

"—you look exactly fucking like him," he said, finishing anyway.

A young gal stepped out of the women's locker room and crossed between us, hair wet and dressed in a business suit. She left behind a vapor trail of fine shampoo, soap and womanliness. We both casually watched her go.

"We're pigs, you know," said Clarke.

"No, we're old men. We're allowed to look at the ladies. It's a privileged we've earned. They know we're harmless. Hell, I think they even like it."

"Like it or not, I saw her glance your way as she passed."

"Maybe she likes old men with chin dimples," I said.

"Except you don't really look like an old man. I mean you're older, but, but you still look like a movie star."

"I *am* a movie star."

"You *were* a movie star."

"Same thing."

"Either way, you still kind of look like one. People think they know you from somewhere and it drives them fucking crazy."

"Not to mention I happen to be cute," I said.

"Let's change the subject," he said.

"Good."

Clarke cranked out another ten reps from the bench machine. I probably should have done another set from the shoulder press, but my shoulder was aching a little. For all the compliments, I was still seventy-four, and these old shoulders weren't getting any younger.

When Clarke was finished, with his lightning vein throbbing, he said, "So how's the case coming along?"

I caught him up to speed, ending with Flip and his twin brother tricking Miranda into sex in high school.

"You're reaching," said Clarke when I had finished.

"I have nothing else to reach for," I said.

"He was just a high school sweetheart."

"Not exactly a sweetheart," I said. "He was willing to give her to his brother for a night."

"So he's charitable," said Clarke. "Either way, I don't see how it relates to the case."

"It doesn't," I said, "except for one thing."

"She still kept the letters," said Clarke, nodding.

"That," I said, "and that he's dead."

Clarke raised his eyebrows. "Dead?"

"Yes."

"Tell me about it."

I did. After leaving Dana's home, I went back to my crime fighting headquarters, or my apartment, and did some research. I ran Flip Barowski's name through one of my industry data bases, privy only to police and private eyes, and, surprise of all surprises, only one Flip Barowski came up. And the one who came up, came up dead. And not just dead, but murdered. A single gunshot wound to the back of the head. Execution style. Two weeks ago to this day. Four days before Miranda's disappearance.

"Could be a coincidence," Clarke said.

"Could be," I said.

"But you don't think so."

"No," I said. "I don't. But, then again, I've been wrong before."

CHAPTER FORTY

I'd performed for presidents and royalty, in packed stadiums and concert venues around the world, and yet when I stepped into the Pussycat for rehearsal that afternoon there were butterflies in my stomach unlike any I had ever experienced. I wanted to puke, go home, and drink myself into oblivion. Exactly in that order.

It was only three-thirty in the afternoon, and the bar was mostly empty, although there was a young couple sitting discretely together, their knees touching, each drinking from their own bottles of beer. I figured them to be tourists, judging by their distinct lack of tans.

The handsome bartender smiled brightly at me when he saw me. "Hey, it's Mr. Johnny Cash," he said, and reached his hand over the counter and shook mine. "Welcome back."

If only he knew.

"Wouldn't be here if it wasn't for you," I said. "Thanks again."

"Hey, man, all you needed was a nudge. Trust me, you did all the rest."

A female customer came in behind me and sat at the bar. The young bartender nodded to her, winked at me, and went back to work. I continued on through the nightclub and headed toward the stage near the back, where Becky was sitting at her piano and flipping through a songbook.

"Hi there, pretty mama," I said, after stepping up onto the stage.

She looked up and smiled and hopped to her feet. She moved quickly around the piano and gave me a world-class hug. I love world-class hugs, especially from pretty young pianists. She kissed me lightly on the cheek, Hollywood style. Her lips felt nice, and her touch felt nicer. There's an inherent camaraderie among musicians, young or old, and it was something I had missed for far too long.

Well, not anymore, dammit.

"You look like hell, King," she said.

"I love you, too," I said.

She grinned easily. She was beautiful in a sort of asexual, sisterly sort of way. Sorry, guys. I mean she seemed to have all the goods, pretty face, long blond hair, and a petite frame. But she wasn't sexy. Perhaps she was too petite. Perhaps she dressed too conservatively. Perhaps I shouldn't give a damn since I was fifty years her senior.

"Don't take it personally, King. I'm just f-ing with you."

She took my hand and led me to the piano bench and sat me down next to her. Our legs touched and, asexual or not, a shiver of pleasure coursed through me.

Focus, King. And quit acting like a schoolboy.

"I got your email," she said, "And I like your taste in music."

"Do you know the songs?"

"Like the back of my hand," she said. "And you're obviously quite fond of Tom Jones."

"One of the greatest performers I've ever seen."

She grinned. "Yeah, I like him, too," she said. "You also have a lot of Neil Diamond in there."

"Neil was an old friend." *Shit.* The moment the words came out, I realized my mistake. *Easy on the name-dropping, big guy.* "Well, *friends* might be too strong of a word. We chatted a few times back in the day. Now we're just Facebook friends, although he won't stop sending me all those damn Farmville requests."

I could feel her eyes on me, scanning every square inch of my face, no doubt racking her brain for some memory of me. If my plastic surgery held up, there wouldn't be any memory to trigger. Finally, she said, "You're funny, King. You ready to work through the set today?"

My stomach did a double flip.

"As ready as I'll ever be," I said.

"Relax. I have a feeling you aren't going to need a lot of practice."

"We'll see."

And so I sat there by her side, our legs touching, and sang a set of fourteen songs, and when we were done, with my voice nearly hoarse and my spirit hovering somewhere near the ceiling, I looked around and saw that we had attracted a small crowd at the base of the stage.

"It's only rehearsal," she said, patting my hand, "and already they love you."

CHAPTER FORTY-ONE

I pulled out of my gated apartment complex and immediately picked up a tail. No, not that kind of tail. A green Intrepid pulled away from the street and followed me down the hill, and proceeded to follow me all the way to Larchmont Street, about six miles away. Coincidence? I think not.

I pulled into a spot in front of Chevalier's Bookstore, and the green Intrepid pulled into a spot about five rows down and across the street. The driver was male. He wore sunglasses and had short brown hair and that's all I knew.

I pulled out my cell phone and called a PI research service of mine. I punched my way through the phone system and soon got a live operator. I gave him my pin and password, then gave him the Intrepid's license plate number. Five minutes later, I had a name. Or, rather, a business name.

The vehicle was owned by the Keys Agency. I knew of the Keys Agency. They were a rival private investigation agency here in L.A. I thought about that a little and then stepped out of my car.

My non-exclusive and Jewish girlfriend calls this area Jew Town, and she was very nearly correct. On any given Friday, you will see conservative Orthodox practitioners with their tassels and braided hair, casually strolling down the streets, forsaking their vehicles in the name of piety.

Perhaps I should forsake booze in the name of piety.

Or not.

I stepped out of my Cadillac and onto the crowded sidewalk that ran along in front of posh stores and upscale restaurants. Most of the shoppers tended to be lovely ladies with little dogs and big sunglasses. Most of the lovely ladies ignored me. Most, but not all. I still garnered one or two looks of curiosity, and maybe one or two of mild interest. Either way, I wasn't used to being ignored, even after thirty years. Hell, I was used to hordes of fans everywhere. I was used to fine food and famous friends and fancy cars.

Today, I was dressed in a polo shirt, cargo shorts with a hammer loop, no hammer; white Van tennis shoes, no socks. Cool, man. My longish brown/gray hair was slicked back. Some stray strands hung loose and dangled over my forehead and cheekbones. Yeah, the cheekbones are still there.

I found him sitting at an outdoor table on the corner of Larchmont and Beverly, and recognized him immediately. The thick neck, the strong jaw, the short buzz cut. He could have stepped straight out of his high school year book. As I approached, weaving my way through a sea of yipping dogs and small saplings growing straight up from sidewalk planters, he didn't bother to look up. In fact, he didn't bother to do much of anything. He just sat there, shoulders slumped, head low, an air of deep melancholy surrounding him. Hell, just seeing him made me want to run to Dr. Vivian, who I may or may not be in love with. I'm leaning towards *maybe*.

I pulled out a metal chair, scraping it noisily over the gum-stained concrete, and sat across from him. He looked up finally.

"Bryan Barowski?" I said.

"You got him," he said.

"I'm sorry about your brother," I said.

"So am I."

"Can I get you something to drink or eat?"

"No, thanks."

"Would you like to move to a quieter spot?" We were on a fairly busy street corner, heavy with traffic and pedestrians.

"I'd rather not."

"Okay," I said.

His eyes dropped down, looking at nothing.

"Thank you for meeting me," I said.

He said nothing, although he might have nodded.

"I lost a twin brother, too," I said.

He inhaled deeply and made a small noise.

I continued. "It was long ago. He died at birth, but he was my brother for nine months and sometimes I can still feel him touching me."

And then Bryan started to cry. Right there in front of the bagel restaurant, his chin pressed into his chest, weeping silently, his body convulsing ever-so-lightly.

* * *

We were now in my car, both eating ice creams. Mine was chocolate malt crunch and his was straight-up vanilla. We both chose waffle cones, which, really, is the only way to go when you're eating ice cream. The investigator in the green Intrepid was watching us behind his big cop glasses. I think he even took a photograph or two. I hate having my picture taken.

"We fucked up," he was saying. "We shared everything."

"And you wanted to share her, too."

"Weird, I know." He slurped his rapidly melting vanilla. "Like I said, we fucked up, and then they broke up, and, I swear, Flip was never the same since."

"He missed her that bad?"

"Yeah. There's something about that girl."

"She's beautiful," I said. My ice cream was dripping faster than I could lick it. I've had worse problems.

"Yeah, there's that, but there's something else." He thought about what that something else was, working his tongue absently around his cone. "She honestly didn't know how pretty she was, how appealing she was, how amazing she was."

"We should all be so lucky."

"No kidding. I begged him just to give me five minutes alone with her."

"Were you going to have sex with her?"

"I think so, yes. I wanted her, and I was so excited. I thought my brother and I could pull it off."

"But she knew the difference?"

"Yeah. Immediately. Right when we started kissing."

"What did she do?"

"She screamed."

"What did you do next?"

"I tried to get her to stop screaming."

"How?"

"Any way I could. I grabbed her and held her down and put my hands over her mouth." His voice trailed off.

"Did you rape her?"

He said nothing, but I could hear him breathing wetly through his nose.

"Did you rape her, Bryan?"

"I don't remember."

We were silent for a long time. My own breathing was nearly as loud as Bryan's, amplified in the cab of my car. I decided to let it drop for now.

"What happened next, Bryan?"

"She grabbed her stuff and ran out."

"What did your brother say?"

"He never forgave me. I mean, it had all been my idea...I had pestered the hell out of him."

"He didn't have to agree."

"Yes, he did. I was relentless."

We both were racing time with our ice creams. My fingers were beyond sticky and now I was getting damn thirsty. Bryan's forehead was beaded with sweat, and I think I was melting into my seat cushions.

I said, "She never wanted anything to do with him again."

"Never again."

I was finishing the last of my cone. Chocolate was between my fingers, down my wrist. Sigh. My little napkin was in tatters.

"And your brother was never the same."

He looked at the rest of his ice cream, opened his door a crack and chucked it out onto the hot street.

"Yeah, never the same," he said.

"He blame you?"

"Of course."

"He loved her?"

"With all of his heart."

Tears were in his eyes. His twin brother of twenty-two years was dead just a few weeks removed. Bryan was holding up well, although I suspected he could crash at any moment.

"And to your knowledge they never saw each other again?" I asked.

"Outside of random meetings at school, not that I know of."

"And you would know," I said.

"Yeah, he couldn't keep anything from me."

Bryan was breathing heavily through his nose. The green car was still there, although the driver was gone. Bryan needed a hug but I wasn't the guy to give it to him.

"You mentioned there was something about this girl," I said.

"Yes."

"Lots of boys at your school liked her?"

"And probably some girls, too."

I smiled. "What about you?"

"Yeah, I liked her."

"Were you jealous that your brother had her and you didn't?"

"Sometimes, yeah."

"Were you jealous that she took time away from you and your brother?"

"Sure. Yeah."

"And your brother still thought about her, even after all these years?"

"I'm sure he did. He didn't talk about it much, but he still loved her."

"Did you love her, too?" I asked.

"No, not like that."

"But you were infatuated with her, like the other guys—and some girls—in school."

"Yeah, something like that."

"Is there a chance your brother might have been seeing her recently?"

He looked at me sharply.

"Why would you say that?" he asked.

"Your brother was murdered, and a few days later Miranda disappeared. That might not be a coincidence."

"I—I don't know. We don't live with each other, so I dunno. But I think I would have known."

"But is there a chance that he could have been seeing her without your knowledge?"

"Maybe, but I would have eventually known."

"How would you have known?"

"I just would have. It's a twin thing. He couldn't keep anything from me."

"Earlier, you said he seemed happier recently."

"Yes."

"Maybe he was happier because he was seeing her," I said.

He shrugged and said nothing. We were both silent and I knew I was upsetting the poor kid, but I also felt that I was onto something here. What it was, I didn't know.

"Why would someone kill your brother?" I asked gently. There was no easy way to do this. You just plunged in and hoped for the best. I knew the facts of the case by now. Detective Colbert, after being bribed with more donuts, had agreed to fax me the preliminary police report. Flip had been found in his car outside a nightclub, dead. Shot once behind the ear. The police had no suspects and very little clues. From all indications, it had been a professional hit.

"I have no idea."

"Was he behaving any differently?"

"I don't know. If anything, he seemed happier. But like I said, we don't live together, so I don't know for sure. I moved out when I was nineteen and he stayed at home."

"Was it hard living away from your brother?"

"Very hard, but you get used to it."

I could not find it within myself to torture the kid a minute longer. His twin was dead, and he himself would never be the same again, and a part of my heart went out to him, even though I was convinced he had raped Miranda. I gave him my card and told him to call me if something came up. He nodded, opened the door, and left. As he did so, I saw that his ice cream had melted into oblivion.

I also saw that the green Intrepid was gone, too.

CHAPTER FORTY-TWO

"They shared everything," I said to Dr. Vivian.

"Twins tend to do that," she said. "At least initially. Later in life, they will outgrow the need for shared experiences."

"Do twins share girls, too?" I asked.

She thought about that. "Depends on the extent of the twins' bond," she said.

"I think the kid was horny and wanted to bop a hot chick," I said.

"It's easy to assume that because that's the obvious answer."

"Then what's the non-obvious answer?" I asked.

"As identical twins, they've had similar—if not identical—experiences. Because of that, they expect to *continue* having identical experiences. And if one of them has something that the other doesn't—"

"The other expects to have it, too," I said, cutting her off. "Except there was only one of Miranda."

"Which is why twins, especially early on through high school and college, will often date other twins. Life is easier that way. Manageable. It makes sense to them. The world is complete, whole. Right. Symmetrical."

It was mid-afternoon. The east-facing window was in shadows, the sun hidden somewhere west of the house. The soft glow from the desk lamp highlighted her sharp chin and equally sharp nose. I wanted to nuzzle that chin, sharp or not.

"I think that, if my own twin had lived," I heard myself saying, "I think—maybe—I would have done anything for him, too. Anything to make him happy."

"That is often the case. Twins will do anything for each other."

"Even share a girl?"

"If that's what it takes to make the other happy, yes," she said.

"The twin that is lacking feels entitled to what the other has."

"Exactly."

"And this has been your personal experience, as well?" I asked.

"Yes, but you outgrow some of it, although not entirely."

"But a high school student…"

"A high school student would still be in the thick of it, and still be confused and prone to make poor decisions."

"Like allowing his brother to have sex with his girlfriend."

"Yes, that would be a poor decision."

The clock above me ticked loudly in the darkened office. I knew that Dr. Vivian lived alone. I knew that she had never been married and I knew that her twin was indeed married. I wondered if Dr. Vivian felt entitled to have sex with her twin's husband. I decided that it was probably best not to ask.

"His twin was murdered," I said.

"So you've said."

"What will happen to him now, being the surviving twin?" I asked.

"He's in serious trouble."

"What do you mean?"

"We might lose him. Drugs, depression, suicide. Pick one. His brother's loss may be too much for him to bear, too much to deal with. In the least, he should probably be under careful supervision."

"What would you do if you lost your sister?" I asked.

"Mr. King…."

"Aaron," I said.

She closed her mouth and tilted her head a little. Her jawline looked sharp enough to cut paper. Sharp but delicate. Her thick glasses gleamed.

"Aaron, that is an awful thought to think, perhaps the worst I can imagine."

We were silent. We watched each other.

"Do twins kill each other?" I asked.

"It happens, but it's rare."

"What would provoke a twin to do that?"

"The usual reasons, but more often than not it stems from jealousy. One twin has amounted to something great, while the other has fallen off the map, so to speak. Even still, something must trigger the killing. A fight, an argument, something. Like I said, it's rare."

"But not out of the question."

"Nothing is out of the question."

"And the twin who does the murdering...?"

"Is screwed forever. The grief is off the charts. The guilt is unbearable." She looked at me for a second or two. "Do you think this boy killed his brother?"

"I don't know," I said. "But either way, he's in trouble."

She nodded. "The suicide rate for surviving twins is off the charts." She looked at me steadily. "And this should give you some indication as to the depth of your own loss, Aaron."

Ah, my own loss. Little Jessie....

"But I don't remember him," I said.

"Yes, you do," she said with surprising urgency. "The memory of your brother is within you, stored away, and can be triggered by any number of techniques."

I knew of a technique, although I sometimes wondered if it was just my imagination. Sometimes when I am alone—especially in bed and especially in the wee hours of morning—I can hear a tiny, frenetic heartbeat, a beautiful sound that surrounds me and fills me. And when this happens, I just lie there and close my eyes and recede deep into my subconscious and slip into a tiny and warm and inviting place. And sometimes...sometimes I have the ghostly sensation of little fingers exploring my little body, touching my head, my cheek, my arm, my leg...and if I am lucky, if I am really lucky, sometimes I can feel this loving little creature hold me close, wrapping his tiny arms and legs around me, and our hearts beat as one and I can feel all the love in the world radiate from this perfect little angel....

And then the sensation would pass and I would lie there in the morning, alone and in agony and weeping.

"I miss him," I said to Dr. Vivian. "I miss him so damn much."

She said nothing, but there were tears in her eyes.

CHAPTER FORTY-THREE

The package was once again delivered via UPS. It was left on my doorstep, propped against my apartment door. UPS and I have this agreement: they keep my signature on file and leave all packages at my door when I'm not home, and I don't throw a shit-fit. It's a nice agreement.

Once again, the package was addressed to E.P. I studied the writing. Small, neat writing. Could be anyone, but more than likely my gig was up, unless I found this person. Unless I convinced them to keep this secret of mine under wraps. The convincing part could turn ugly.

I unlocked the door, tossed my keys on my kitchen table, and immediately opened the small package. Inside was a compact disk. I pulled it out and turned it over.

Son-of-a-bitch.

It was my daughter's latest album. In fact, it wasn't even in the stores yet. A pirated copy, perhaps. A red disclaimer in the bottom corner read: *Advanced Copy—Resale Strictly Prohibited,* followed by penalties and fines, which included more money than I had in my savings and checking combined. Oh, and jail time, too.

So who had sent it? And why? Obviously someone who worked within the music industry, right? Or perhaps the CD had been stolen. In fact, more than likely it had been stolen.

My heart thumping loudly in my chest, I looked at my daughter's picture on the CD cover. God, she was beautiful. And she was certainly my baby. We had the same eyes and lips, only my eyes and lips looked far different now. She looked happy in this picture, real joy in her eyes and in her smile. Daddy was proud.

So was this CD sent as a direct threat against my daughter? A warning? Was something going to happen to her? What the fuck was going on?

I went to the fridge and popped a Miller Lite and drank it right there in front of the open refrigerator. I tossed the empty bottle, popped open another, and brought it and the disk over to the CD player.

I inserted the disk and pressed *play*.

CHAPTER FORTY-FOUR

Hours later, long after I had listened to my daughter's newest CD more times than I could remember, my feet were up on the old artist drawing table that doubled as my desk, and I was deep in thought.

Kendra the Wonder Kat was up on the desk, too, next to the keyboard, sleeping on an afghan blanket that I had folded there for her. She was curled in a tight ball, her black tiger stripes prominent against her gray fur. She spasmed slightly in her sleep, perhaps dreaming of chasing mice or rubber superballs.

Through my open sliding glass door, a mishmash of trees and plants and everything in-between swayed and swished on the hillside that rose up just outside my balcony. Beyond the trees, mostly hidden from sight, were Echo Park's bigger homes. Beyond them was Elysian Park, and still further was Dodger Stadium.

I was trying to make sense of the facts of the case, and nothing much was making sense. I had a dead twin, a missing girl, a white van, an unknown driver, a bum, a grocery store clerk, a distraught mother, and little else.

Actually there *was* something else. I went online and found a number in the Yahoo Yellow Pages. I dialed it and while I waited, I scratched my sleeping cat between her ears. She mewed and stretched and then sort of curled under herself in a position that didn't look entirely comfortable, but one she seemed fine with. The line picked up.

"Keys Agency."

"Rick Keys please."

"You got him."

"Help, I think my wife is cheating on me!"

"I'm sorry to hear that, what makes you—"

"You were following me the other day, dickhead," I said, breaking in. "I want to know why."

Rick was silent, chewing on this. "Is this King?"

"You think?"

"Just doing my job, King. No hard feelings."

"Who hired you?"

"You know I can't tell you that."

"I could threaten to kick your ass," I said.

"You're too old to kick my ass."

"True," I said, but I still thought I could take him. Keys was smaller than I, and he wore a mustache. I could kick anyone's ass who wore a mustache. "Then what was the nature of the surveillance?"

I could almost hear him working through it on the other end of the line. I had, after all, tagged him. The gig was up.

"To follow you," he said. "And give a detailed report of your activity."

"And did you?"

"Emailed it this morning," he said. "And about an hour ago I was called off your case."

"Called off?"

"The assignment is over."

"You must have filed a hell of a report."

"Or that I inadvertently gave my client what they were looking for."

"And you won't tell me who this person is?"

"Not even if you beat me with your cane. Goodbye, King."

He hung up, and I absently drummed my finger on my unsteady drawing desk, which promptly started wobbling. Someday I would get a new desk. Someday. But new desks cost money, and I'd become a miser in my dotage.

Wobbling or not, the cat slept soundly, although her ears moved independently of each other, no doubt honing in on police sirens, bird chirps and sounds unheard by human ears.

So who had hired Keys to follow me? I didn't know, but I took it as a sign that I was getting close to the truth, and if I had to, I'd beat the shit out of Keys to get his information.

Better go buy a cane.

CHAPTER FORTY-FIVE

"Flip what's-his-name's murder and Miranda's disappearance could still be a coincidence," said Clarke.

"That's no way to speak of the dead."

"Coming from someone who's supposed to be dead."

We were in my apartment. I was sitting at my desk drinking a beer and absently flipping through Miranda's case file. Clarke was making his rounds around my apartment again; meaning, he was examining everything, touching everything and generally acting a bit creepy. He did this sometimes, and I wasn't sure why. I knew that Clarke had been a big fan of mine, but he usually kept his fan-like tendencies in check. Except on these rare occasions when he seemed incapable of sitting still, when he seemed possessed by a need to peruse my home, my belongings, my everything. I was certain—and this was a slightly disturbing thought—that he would have probably gone through my drawers if I were not around. Not that he would take anything, just that he seemed incapable of controlling himself, of reigning himself in.

At the moment, he was standing in front of my entertainment center, looking at the assorted pictures of my daughter and caressing the frames carefully. I wondered if he was even aware of his actions.

"Do the police have any leads on his murder?" Clarke asked.

"None yet."

"Or none that they're telling you."

"Or that," I said.

"So he gets murdered and four days later she goes missing. We still don't even know if they were dating, let alone seeing each other. Might be good to know."

I agreed.

Now Clarke was looking at my shot glass chess set carefully. Picking up each piece, turning the glasses over in his fingers, and putting them back exactly where he had found them. Disturbing as it was, I was used to this strange behavior, and just chalked it up as another bizarre oddity in the life and times of Aaron King and his attorney sidekick, Clarke.

Miranda's case file was now quite thick and filled mostly with my own hand-written notes, all stamped, of course, with the date they were filed and placed in chronological order. A private detective's notes can potentially be subpoenaed and used in a court of law, and so I did everything by the book, just in case I was ever called in to testify, which I sometimes was. I generally made for a good witness, in part because of my meticulous notes.

And because you are a ham.

Now as I flipped through the file, skimming past notes and witness statements and tidbits of evidence collected no matter how small or trivial, I came across a tiny piece of paper that I had taped to a bigger piece of paper so that it wouldn't get lost in the shuffle. It was the receipt I had found in Miranda's jeans. I squinted at it now. A pub called Half Pint. It was in Hollywood, and I knew the place. The receipt was dated two days *before* Flip's murder and, consequently, six days before Miranda's disappearance.

Presently, Clarke was scanning the books on my bookshelf—the same books he had scanned a few weeks earlier, the last time he was here. He pulled one out, leafed through it, shoved it back in place. Now he was examining the DVD covers to Miranda's movies. The movies were days late, but I didn't care. I would add the fines to my final bill.

As I watched Clarke flip through the movies, an idea occurred to me, and as it did a familiar sensation rippled through me. It was my Spidey-sense, so to speak. It told me that I was in the presence of a clue, or perhaps something big. Either that, or I had eaten some bad shrimp for lunch.

"Clarke, you've seen all of Miranda's movies, right?"

"Of course," he said. He had already moved on to examining my dented brass world globe. "I'm an entertainment attorney, remember? I represent Miranda and her family, and I get free shit all the time, especially movies and CDs, sometimes even before they come out."

"Fine," I said. "What were the themes of the first two movies?"

"Themes?"

"You know, the basic through-line?"

He tilted his head, thinking, then moved away from the globe and re-read the back of the movies. "A bank heist and a serial killer."

"Look deeper," I said.

He did, then snapped his head up.

"She was kidnapped in both," he said.

I nodded and stood. I ran my hand through my hair, my mind racing, and paced the small area in font of my computer desk. There was something here. Something important.

"So what are you getting at, Aaron?"

"I'm not sure yet," I said.

"You think someone kidnapped her?"

"I don't know."

"Life imitating art?"

"Maybe. There's something here. I can feel it."

"You're grasping at straws."

"At least I'm grasping at *something*."

"Millions of people have seen her movies, Aaron. That's a lot of potential suspects."

"So let's narrow it," I said. "What do we know about Miranda?"

"And that's a rather broad ques—"

I cut him off. "We know that the men in her life tend to act oddly, irrationally."

Clarke nodded, following me.

"She tends to attract stalkers," he said.

"And those who appear to have a hard time letting her go," I said.

"Like her ex-boyfriend," said Clarke.

"Exactly."

"So you're saying some weirdo watched these two movies, developed an obsession with her, and decided to act out the movies and kidnap her?"

"Maybe. I don't know."

"That's a hell of a reach, my friend."

I ignored him. "What if Miranda found herself in another situation where someone she knew or dated is having a hard time letting go," said Clarke.

"By keeping her captive, like in the movies?"

"Maybe it's a sick fantasy."

"I'll bite, but unless it's someone she knows, that's a lot of potential suspects out there."

"Then let's work with who she knows."

"Hey, you're the detective, Aaron. I'm just a humble entertainment attorney." He finally sat on the leather sofa, which he examined as well, running his hands over it and basically molesting the thing. "We know all about her past boyfriends. One's dead, and one's in New York. So who's left?"

I had stepped over to the DVD cases and was flipping through them, thinking hard. "Is there anything else that connects her with these two movies?" I asked.

"What do you mean?"

"Did she work with the same actors or director?"

Clarke shook his head.

"No, I repped her for both deals. Different directors and actors." He frowned and stopped examining my couch. "But she did sign a two-movie deal with Alpha-Beta Productions."

"So she worked with the same producers on both movies?"

"Exactly."

"But not on her third or fourth movie?"

Clarke nodded. "Right. She'd left Alpha-Beta by then and was working with a new production company."

That familiar tingle was back, that wonderful crackle that whipped wildly through my body like an electric current. Now I was about 90% certain it wasn't the shrimp I had eaten at lunch.

"So maybe someone from her old production studio didn't want her to leave?" said Clarke.

"Maybe," I said.

"Another obsession?"

"Only one way to know."

CHAPTER FORTY-SIX

Half Pint was a small place in Hollywood. It was also gloomy and consisted mostly of a lot of tall stools and one long scarred oak counter. A massive screen TV hung suspended from the ceiling. Presently showing on it was a taped Joe Cocker concert. Lord, I love that man.

I sat on a tall stool at the long bar. The bartender was a young guy with a lot of hair and even more tattoos. He wore his jeans low on his hips. There was something shiny sticking out of his chin. A spike, I think. I ordered a Heineken and showed him the picture of Miranda. As he poured my drink, he studied the picture closely, squinting.

"Beautiful girl," he said.

"She ever drink here?"

He frowned, which for some reason caused the spike in his chin to turn up a little. "Looks a little familiar."

"She was here two weeks ago," I said.

"Why do you care?"

I told him why I cared, that she was missing and quite possibly dead, and showed him my PI license. He squinted at my picture. Frowned some more. The spike in his chin quivered.

"What day was she here again?" he asked.

I told him the date on the receipt. He went over to a dirty calendar hanging on a wall near a door behind the bar. He pealed back a page and scanned the dates with his finger. As he did so, he unconsciously pushed his lower teeth out against his bottom lip. The movement projected the spike forward, making it look like a mini warhead ready to launch from his face.

He came back and stood in front of me. More frowning. More quivering. I found the spike highly distracting.

"Yeah," he said. "I worked that night. Mind if I see the picture again?"

I showed him it again and he studied it some more and began nodding. The spike nodded, too. Damn that spike.

"Yeah, I remember her. Hard to forget that face, come to think of it."

"That's what they all say."

"Seriously. She had everyone here going."

"Who's everyone?"

"Another bartender, the bus boys, some of the local chaps."

"Did she do anything to get you boys going?"

"Didn't have to. Just sitting here was enough."

"She that pretty?" I asked.

"Look for yourself."

I did, again, for the millionth time.

"She's a real looker," I said.

"That's an understatement."

"So what did she do when she was here?"

"She ordered a glass of wine, paid for it with cash, and then a guy comes in and sits next to her. We all sort of groaned, you know. The lucky son of a bitch."

Ah, the plot thickens.

"Could you describe the guy?"

"Sure, we all checked him out. You know, the old 'what's he got that we don't?' sort of thing."

"So what did he have that you didn't?"

"Muscles. Thick neck."

I showed the bartender another picture. The bartender took one look at it and nodded. "Yup, that's him."

It was Flip Barowski, of course.

"Can you tell me what they did together?" I asked.

"Talked—and lots of it. The guy seemed upset, or something. Not necessarily at her, you see. He was talking—" he searched for the right word, "—excitedly."

"Like perhaps he was trying to get her to forgive an egregious error."

The bartender grinned and the missile in his lip turned up. T-minus and counting....

"Sure, something like that," he said and grinned again.

"Did they kiss, hold hands, any public displays of affection?"

He was nodding. "Yeah, I noticed his hand in her lap, but that was it. And then they left together and I haven't seen them since."

And he wouldn't, either.

CHAPTER FORTY-SEVEN

A true multi-tasker, I went from the pub straight to my next appointment.

I was early for the appointment, but I didn't care. *I'm a rebel like that.* Besides, I was giddy with excitement. I hadn't been to the Paramount lot in nearly forty years. I doubted the old crew was still there, and if anyone was, they sure as hell wouldn't know who I was, not now. Besides, I had just been a kid back then, determined and full of ambition. Paramount had given me my first movie break, and so, no matter what had happened after, they would always have a special place in my heart.

I pulled up to the pearly gates. Or, in this case, the massive wrought-iron gates right off Melrose Avenue. The security guard was packing heat. Movies are serious business.

"Name?" he said.

Elvis Presley.

"Aaron King," I said.

He scanned his list, found my name, checked it off with a pen that had been tucked behind his ear. He gave me a parking permit that I placed between my dash and windshield. A moment later, the red-striped arm barrier rose. Access granted.

I drove slowly down a center road, passing between buildings and offices and sound stages. An entire street straight out of the Bronx appeared to my left, a beautiful replication of downtown living. Pedestrians were strolling up and down the thing as if it were the real deal. Maybe they were replications, as well. Movie magic.

My appointment was with Alpha-Beta Productions, the same company that had produced Miranda's first two movies. The same movies which just so happened to feature her being kidnapped.

I eventually found Alpha-Beta's building in the back corner of the lot. It was a massive, ivy-covered brick structure that didn't look entirely structurally sound. It was also a building I was certain I had visited many years before, and under very different circumstances, of course.

I made movies here. My *own* first movies.

I turned off the car and stepped outside. There are few places on earth like a major Hollywood studio; truly worlds unto their own. I breathed in the surprisingly fresh air, air only marginally tainted with combustion and smog. This was Hollywood air. *Magic air.* Movies were created here, real movie magic, magic I had once been a part of. Those movies, no matter how campy, had put a lot of smiles on a lot of faces—as they would continue to do so—and, really, what more could you ask?

I stood there, next to my car, turning slowly, taking in what I could, knowing there was much more hidden from view, secret chambers and rooms and stages where the magic further happened.

Maybe I'll make a movie again.

As Aaron King.

Lord, help me.

I stopped scanning and I think my jaw dropped a little. Actually, I was certain my jaw had dropped. There, just around the corner of Alpha-Beta's brick building, was a fleet of white vans. White cargo vans. Five of them to be exact, all no doubt used to transport props, supplies and people to various sets and stages.

Milton the bum had seen a white cargo van, driven by a man with pockmarks. There's a million white cargo vans in L.A, of course. Hell, there's probably a hundred or so white cargo vans here on this lot.

I think this was a clue.

CHAPTER FORTY-EIGHT

Heart thumping steadily in my old chest, I stepped into the Alpha-Beta offices and was greeted by a pretty young thing sitting behind a kidney-shaped desk. By greeted, I mean stared at blankly. The pretty young thing was wearing ultra-hip rectangular glasses that made her blank stare look even more blank. She asked if she could help me. I told her she could. She waited. I waited. She then asked *how* she could help me. I told her how, that I had an appointment to see Gregory Ladd, owner of the company. She asked for my name and I gave it to her. She tried to contain her enthusiasm. One of her techniques for containing her enthusiasm was to push her narrow glasses up the bridge of her nose and stare at me blankly some more.

Now, what if I had said Elvis Presley? I wondered. *Well, she would have laughed or called security. Elvis is dead, remember?*

"He's in a meeting," she said dispassionately. I hate dispassionately. "I'll let him know you're here as soon as he's available."

"That would be swell."

And, to my surprise, the empty veneer showed some life. "Did you just say *swell?*" she asked.

"I think so, yes."

"Haven't heard that word in, like, forever."

"It means 'so well'."

"Does it?"

Okay, I made that up. I've been making a lot of things up these past 30 years. What's another white lie?

"Sure," I said, and took a seat near the front door.

She went back to her computer, grinning, and for all I know Googling the root of *swell.* Who knows, maybe I'm right and I'm a genius after all. At least she had smiled, and, dammit, smiles always made me feel good.

Of course, her smile had also made me think of my daughter's smile. And as I waited for Mr. Ladd, I wondered how my baby girl was doing, and I wondered for the millionth time why I wasn't with her and her celebrating her life. *Our* life.

Jesus, what the hell am I doing?

I looked again at the pretty young receptionist, but she was no longer smiling, which was just as well, because now she no longer looked like my little girl. Lost in thoughts of my empty life, I nearly failed to notice the man striding purposefully toward me down a side hallway.

"Aaron King?" he said, appearing before me, sticking out his hand. "I'm Gregory Ladd. Why don't we go back to my office and talk."

I looked up…and nearly gasped. Luckily, I'm a professional. The man standing above me, the man still holding out his hand toward me, was just the man I was looking for. Then again, I've been wrong before.

Not this time, baby.

And so I put on a big fake smile and stood on jelly knees and took the proffered hand and pumped it energetically. Gregory Ladd grinned, which made his badly scarred, pock-marked face significantly less menacing. He led the way back down the hallway to his office.

I followed obediently, my heart pounding somewhere near my throat.

CHAPTER FORTY-NINE

The office wasn't so much an office as a massive open space with a desk in one corner of the room. The rest of the room was comprised of a lot of sofas and overstuffed chairs, and I imagined that the staff of Alpha-Beta had a lot of production meetings in here, hammering out all things to do with the making of movies.

I could also imagine nervous young screenwriters, sweating and stuttering, pitching their movies here. I'd been to such pitch meetings before with young screenwriters, and it's not a pretty sight.

The room was covered with movie posters and bookcases and heavy curtains. The ancient wood floor was badly scarred and rutted, although it had probably been freshly laid and rut-free back when I was here making movies.

It was humbling to know I was older than wood itself. What was next? Dirt? Small hills? Dan Rather?

I was breathing slowly and calmly, or trying to. I was also trying to look cool and collected, and so, again, I reverted back to my acting days—no, not the parts where I break out in song and dance—but the parts where I really gave acting a go. I decided that an inquisitive, professional mask was best, and so, as Ladd stepped around his desk and sat down, I eased into character. Or at least tried to.

He gestured toward one of the cushioned chairs in front of his desk. "Have a seat Mr. King," he said.

As I sat, he rather hastily clicked off a few images from his screen. Unfortunately, I didn't catch what they had been. And, yes, I'm nosy like that. I get paid to be nosy.

His desk was cluttered with tattered scripts, books with broken spines and unmarked DVDs. I hate seeing books with broken spines. Something sort of barbaric about that. Reckless and wasteful. Maybe I had been a writer in a past life. Anyway, he saw me looking at the paperback novels and picked one up.

"We had the author in here last week. A cute little old lady who writes some of the hottest sex scenes you've ever read."

"You got her number?" I asked.

He laughed. "She's a lot older than even you, Mr. King. In her eighties, I think. What are you...fifty, fifty-five?"

"Seventy-one."

"No shit?"

"No shit," I said.

"You're in great shape."

"It's all the salsa dancing I do. Helps burn off the chocolate fudge Ensures."

He was still grinning. "Ensures...that's the old-people protein shake, right?" he said.

"Right."

"You're a funny guy, King, I like that." He sat back and steepled his fingers under his chin. He studied me for a moment or two. The light in this room failed to reach the deeper craters of his acne scars. He looked, in this moment, menacing as hell. "You're here about Miranda Scott."

"Yes," I said.

"Word around town is that she went missing. I assume that's why you're here."

"You assume correctly."

"We're all worried sick here."

I'm sure you are, I thought, but knew that wasn't entirely fair. After all, I wasn't certain Ladd was the guy. Surely there were tens of thousands of men with facial scars in L.A. who had access to white cargo vans, who just so happened to produce two movies that features Miranda being kidnapped. *Not to mention I'm taking the word of a career bum—hardly an iron-clad witness.*

Still, say that to my thumping heart and the rush of adrenaline flooding my blood stream.

Easy, old boy.

"Yes, a difficult time for everyone," I said, proud of my performance. "May I ask what your relationship to Miranda was?"

"I produced her first and second feature. We basically gave her her first shot."

And, perhaps, feel entitled to her? A sort of ownership?

"So you were, in essence, her boss?"

"In essence."

Gregory Ladd was a big man, although not overweight. He looked dense and strong, and if he was pissed off enough he could probably rip the arms off his swivel chair and pound you to death with them. Then again, that could be my overactive imagination at work. For the most part, he avoided direct eye contact with me, which I found odd, especially coming from a big Hollywood executive who made a living making the right connections with the right people. Maybe I was the *wrong* connection.

"Have the police interviewed you?" I asked.

"No," he said, looking at me squarely. "Why would they do that? Our company hasn't worked with Miranda for two years. We officially cut ties. She's already made two other movies with a different studio."

And how about unofficially? I wondered.

Ladd was trying to sound cool. He was trying to sound nonchalant, but I heard it in his voice. It was jealousy. And there was a touch of anger, too. To me it was obvious: he didn't appreciate her leaving his production company.

Ladd was clicking his mouse nervously with his index finger, over and over...the movement was compulsive and revealing and I nearly reached across the desk and grabbed the guy by the throat and demanded that he tell me where the hell Miranda was, but I knew that would be a mistake. One, he outweighed me by thirty pounds; two, he was thirty years younger than myself; and three, I just might have choked the life out of him.

Deep breath, big guy.

"What was your personal relationship with Miranda?" I asked.

He shrugged, clicked the mouse. "Typical, I suppose. Saw her on the set. She mostly communicated with the directors."

"So you did not have a personal relationship?"

"We were friends, yes. Many of us would go out drinking after a day's shoot. She and I were friendly, certainly, but when the films wrapped...."

His voice trailed off and I knew the feeling. It was the cruel, unspoken reality of making films. Crash course best friends for three months, then...nothing. Sometimes the friendships lasted into other movies and sometimes into something deep and real, but more often than not the friendship was done along with the completion of the movie. At least, that had been my experience.

"Were you two lovers?" I asked.

He quit clicking and looked slowly up at me. His face, I saw, was unusually and deeply pock-marked. He looked like a hardened criminal. An unfair stereotype, certainly, but one that might be accurate in this case.

"No," he said simply.

"Did you want to be?" I asked.

"You ask a lot of questions."

"When I find Miranda, I'm sure she'll appreciate my thoroughness."

"Well I *don't*," he said. "You're being rude and intrusive."

I said nothing. I wasn't looking for an argument, and I wasn't looking to one-up him with my dazzling wit. I wanted Miranda. I said nothing, and let his emotions play out as I sat there quietly.

"She was a beautiful young woman certainly," he said finally. "Any man would have jumped at the opportunity to be with Miranda."

His words hung in the air and I listened to them again, and again. "You just referred to Miranda in the past tense," I said. "Do you know something that I don't?"

"What the fuck does that mean?"

"You tell me."

"It was just a goddamn slip of the tongue."

"Right," I said. "Could happen to anybody. Do you ever drive those white cargo vans out front?"

"Sure, we all do sometimes. Why?"

"Do you ever shop at Trader Joe's?"

"Rarely. I don't see how that has to do with anything."

"Miranda was kidnapped from a Trader Joe's in a white cargo van. Follow me now?"

He looked at me openly and threateningly. His broad forehead crinkled. He leaned forward a little in his desk. I think I was supposed to shrink back in fear. I didn't shrink.

"I don't like what you're insinuating," he said.

"Hardly anyone would."

"This meeting is over."

"Figured as much," I said.

CHAPTER FIFTY

As I left the Alpha-Beta production offices, I quickly scanned the nearly empty parking lot—and spotted what I had hoped to see: A black Mercedes SL500, with a license plate that read: LADSTER.

Sometimes you just get lucky.

I exited the Paramount lot and turned immediately into a rundown gas station just up the street a little. I parked facing the street, with a good view of the Paramount lot. I bought a couple of Frappuccinos and a small box of Oreos at the station's convenience store, then waited in my car and watched the main exit from Paramount Studios.

It was late afternoon and sweltering. No telling when Ladd might leave, and if he was in the middle of a project, he could potentially be there all night.

Sweat poured from my brow. I finished off the first Frapp-uccino and started on the second. I also started on the Oreos. I was soon buzzing on caffeine and sugar and wishing like hell the convenience store also sold Vicodins.

You got issues, man.

I also thought about Gregory Ladd. He was certainly big enough to abduct Miranda, but that didn't mean much since there didn't appear to be any sort of struggle in the Trader Joe's parking lot. But that didn't mean there hadn't been a struggle, either. Milton the bum wasn't sure what he had seen. First she had been leaving Trader Joe's, and the next thing he knew she was in the van.

He's also a drunk.

Sure, I thought. *But he was there; he had seen something.*

Ladd had been her boss once. Maybe he had a secret crush on her. Maybe he loved her from afar and couldn't stand the fact that she was making movies with someone else. *Or dating her ex-boyfriend again.*

And now that ex-boyfriend was dead.

I tapped my fingers on my super-heated steering wheel. I drank some more of the Frappuccino. Sweat rolled down into my ear. I shivered.

I didn't like how Ladd referred to Miranda in the past tense. As if he knew something had happened to her. As if he *knew* something had happened to her. As if he might be *personally responsible* for something happening to her.

I tapped some more on the steering wheel.

He had been jealous or irritated or angry that she had left his production company to make movies elsewhere, that much was obvious to me. But perhaps it went deeper. Perhaps he *missed* making movies with her. Perhaps he was secretly in love with her.

I didn't know, but I was beginning to think that Miranda was destined to attract the crazies. Perhaps Ladd, like every other male who had crossed paths with her, had fallen victim to her charm and beauty. But he, unlike the others, had taken things a step further.

Like kidnap?

Maybe.

My cell rang. I looked at the faceplate and saw that it was Miranda's mother, Dana Scott. I flipped it open.

"Miss Scott," I said.

"Mr. King, this is Dana Scott."

"I would never have guessed."

But she wasn't listening, or, more likely, she couldn't quite hear me.

"You there, King?" she asked.

"I'm here."

"...barely hear...."

Sigh. I sat up straighter and held the phone out at a different angle, hoping that this would somehow help the reception. Amazingly, it did.

"Can you hear me now?" I asked.

"Yes, there you are," she said, her voice coming in sharp and clear. "Mr. King, I'm calling you off the case."

"Excuse me?"

"Your services are no longer needed, Mr. King."

"Has Miranda been found?"

"No."

"Then how could my services no longer be needed?"

"Did I or did I not hire you?"

"You did."

"Then I can fire you as I see fit."

"That's certainly your prerogative, yes."

"Then consider yourself fired, Mr. King."

"How about no."

"What does that mean?"

"It means I don't consider myself fired."

"Are you misunderstanding me?"

"Probably not."

"You're fired, Mr. King."

"I disagree," I said. "At least tell me why—"

"Just get off the fucking case," she screamed, cutting me off, and had her phone been an old-fashioned phone she would have slammed it down. Instead, she merely clicked off vehemently.

I snapped shut my phone and wondered what the hell had just happened.

CHAPTER FIFTY-ONE

Two hours and another box of Oreos later, the black Mercedes SL500 finally exited the studio gates and hung a right. I almost cheered. I knew my relieved stomach did. I fumbled for the keys, gunned the car, and whipped out of the gas station, hanging what could only be described as a suicidal left turn onto Melrose. Cars honked, tires squealed, and somehow I made it out of the gas station alive.

Way to stay inconspicuous, King.

Luckily, this was L.A. and honking horns were the norm. Once settled in traffic, and ignoring the glares and fingers of the recently cut-off, I eased close enough to the Mercedes to verify that it was indeed the LADSTER. Once verified, I fell back a few car lengths, and soon discovered that Gregory Ladd was not your typical L.A. driver; meaning, he drove slowly and was generally a peach on the road.

My cell rang again. I snapped it open.

"King," I said.

"King its Keys."

"We sound like a bad mattress commercial," I said.

"Yeah, no shit. Anyway, remember that case we talked about?"

"No, remind me."

"Don't fuck with me, King. I've got something for you."

Ladd hung a right and I followed him north up Vine.

"Go on," I said.

"My client just called me again."

"The one who hired you to follow me."

"Yeah, that one."

"You on the case again?" I asked.

"No, but my client asked for a referral."

"What do you mean?"

"My client asked, rather discreetly I might add, that if I knew of someone who could convince you to stay off a case."

"Convince as in dead?"

"That's how I took it, but then again maybe my client just wants you roughed up a little."

"Hard to rough me up when I've got my cane."

"That's how I figure it," he said.

"So did you give this person what they wanted?"

"Hell, no. I know some shooters, but I don't throw work their way."

"Business and ethics, I'll be damned."

"Look, King. The next guy she calls may not be as morally upstanding as me. The next guy she calls may find someone to do you."

"She?"

"Yeah," he said, and he was silent, or perhaps this was what is called a *pregnant pause*. At any rate, when he was done thinking about it, he said. "Yeah...*she*."

"What's her name?"

"Dana Scott," he said.

I was silent. He was silent. The Mercedes drove steadily on. The early evening was bright and warm. Vine Street was surprisingly quiet, so I dropped far back a few more car lengths without fear of losing Ladd.

"I owe you one," I said.

"Or two," he said, and he hung up.

CHAPTER FIFTY-TWO

Twenty minutes later, the LADSTER turned into Laurel Canyon. Unfortunately, due to the main road being partially washed away by a massive rainstorm last year, Ladd and I—and seemingly all of Los Angeles—were redirected along a narrow side street.

Presently, I was three car lengths behind Ladd, and so far the movie producer made no indication of spotting me. Admittedly, I seemed to have a natural knack for following people. Must be the stalker in me.

While we crawled up the canyon, I worked the phone. First I called Detective Colbert. He seemed overjoyed to hear from me.

"Just the man I wanted to talk to," he said. "But I'm in the middle of something."

"I have a request."

"Can it wait?"

"It's a matter of life and death."

"Who's life?"

"Mine."

"It can wait," he said, and hung up.

Five minutes he called back.

"We've got a body here," he said.

"Whose body?"

"Kid named Bryan Barowski. We found your card in his wallet. You sure get around for an old guy."

But I wasn't really listening and I had no comeback to that. My lungs had stopped working and something inside me seemed to sink down, way down, and it continued sinking.

I heard myself saying: "He killed himself."

"How do you know that?"

"Call it a hunch. How did he do it?"

"Gun to the temple. Left a note. Misses his brother, doesn't want to live without him, made some horrible mistakes, tell his mother goodbye for him, yada yada."

The weight was still there on my heart, on my lungs, and I wanted to pull over and get out of the car and breathe and maybe throw up.

Keep moving forward, King.

"What I don't understand," Colbert was saying, "is why I have to tell his mother that he loves her. Why the fuck couldn't he call her before blowing his brains out?"

But Colbert's merciless voice was getting smaller and smaller, and it was being steadily replaced by a tiny heartbeat. A fast and tiny heartbeat.

"I think I know who killed his brother," I said.

"Who?"

And so I told him.

CHAPTER FIFTY-THREE

Colbert went silent. I thought maybe I had lost him. I checked the phone's connection. I hadn't. Traffic was stopped. Just ahead, a small tractor was slowly reversing into traffic, its scoop full of dirt and debris, busy clearing off the road. A man with a hard hat held up a crossing guard stop sign.

"Miranda's mother?" he finally said. "Dana Scott?"

"Yes."

"You're high, King."

"Often, but not this time."

He didn't laugh, nor did I expect him too. I walked him through Dana's strange behavior, from when she caught me going through Miranda's drawer of letters, to her hiring Keys to follow me, to her relieving Keys of his duty once he had established I made contact with the surviving twin, and to her desire to keep me permanently off the case. I also told him about the stunt the twins had pulled in their teens, which resulted in a rape.

"That was five years ago," said Colbert. "Why does the mother kill Flip Barowski now?"

"He and Miranda were seeing each other again."

"And you know this?"

"Yes."

"You've been busy, King."

"I happen to be an ace detective."

"Whatever," said Colbert. "So he's dating her daughter again, big deal. That still doesn't explain why she kills him."

I heard Dana Scott's words again: "*I told him that if I ever saw him or his fucking perverted brother again, I would kill them both.*"

And now they were both dead. As a parent, I knew I would have said the same thing. Hell, I probably would have followed up on it, too, especially after what the twins did to Miranda. Feeling like a rat, I told Colbert about the threat.

"You think she followed up on her threat?" he asked.

"I think so, yes," I said.

"And then she tried to hire someone to stop you?"

"Appears so."

"So the mother kills the new boyfriend, who is actually the old boyfriend, and then a few days later the daughter disappears."

"Yes," I said.

"I don't see the connection," he said.

"There might not be one, at least not directly related."

"What the hell does that mean, King?"

"I'll tell you when I know more."

"When will you know more?"

"Soon," I said, looking at the LADSTER three cars ahead. "Very soon."

I heard him thinking on the line. I could almost see him shaking his head. Finally, he said, "Fine. Call me as soon as you find out anything."

"You'll be my first call, unless I need an emergency pepperoni pizza from Dominos."

"Make it sausage, and I'll spring for half," he said, and clicked off.

CHAPTER FIFTY-FOUR

The tractor finished clearing the debris from the roadway, and the man in the hard hat flipped his sign around so that it now read SLOW. The long line of cars was moving again and I was giddy with excitement. Sitting in traffic drove me crazy, which is why I taught myself every side street in L.A. Now my motto is: *all roads lead to home.*

We wound slowly up through Laurel Canyon, picking up speed exponentially as vehicles veered off to the many residential side streets. Good for traffic; bad for me. Bad because I would soon be exposed, and that's never a good thing.

When the last of the three cars between Ladd and myself turned into a long driveway, I immediately flipped on my turn signal. A moment later, I hung a right onto a random residential street. Ladd and his SL500 continued up the winding road.

I parked in front of a house along this side street, knowing that Ladd was getting away, but that was okay. Back at the gas station, with some time on my hands and a belly full of Oreos, I had called in Ladd's license plate and fifty bucks later I had his current address. Well, current at least to the DMV.

Since I knew Laurel Canyon like the back of my hand, age spots and all, I knew he was heading home, or somewhere damn close to it. A decade or so ago I had dated a girl who lived up here. A trapeze artist who was just flexible but hyper-flexible, which means she could do the splits and then some. Yawza! Her home was up here, along with her practice equipment, and so on any given day neighbors could see her flying high through the air. I came up here and watched her practice as often as I could, and often caught myself drooling like an imbecile.

Maybe I should look her up someday.

I drummed my fingers on the steering wheel and wondered what I hoped to find at Ladd's house. I didn't know. I hadn't done a thorough background check on the man. He could have been married with five kids. He could have been pleasantly gay with five adopted kids. He didn't look gay, and he hadn't been wearing a wedding ring, and there hadn't been any pictures of kids or wives or girlfriends or boyfriends on his desk. Of course, none of that meant anything, but sometimes it did.

Then again, I could have the wrong guy. After all, I was taking the word of a bum. A dying bum, no less. And was the word *bum* even politically correct these days? *Residentially challenged?*

After ten more minutes, I put my car back into gear and turned back onto the main road, which led deeper into the canyon. Traffic was lighter now, and moving fast. Being an old duffer, I rarely did anything fast, and that included driving.

Tough shit, folks. Reflexes aren't what they used to be. Deal with it.

And they did, by riding my ass all the way to my next turn-off a few miles away, a turn-off that just so happened to be Ladd's street.

CHAPTER FIFTY-FIVE

I drove slowly up the street, which was narrow and curved and rose steadily up into the surrounding hills. My heart, admittedly, was hammering in my chest.

The expensive homes up here were few and far between, their owners paying handsomely for privacy and acreage. Again, good for them, bad for me. As an investigator, sitting in my parked car, I would stand out like an old, wrinkled sore thumb. Well, maybe not *that* wrinkled.

Most of the residences had long driveways, with the houses tucked far back from the road. Sometimes I could just make out some of the houses at the far end of long, curved driveways. Big homes with great views. Big homes with lots of privacy. I understand wanting privacy. I get it.

If a tree falls in the forest, and no one is around to hear it, does it make a sound? Or, in this case, if someone screams, and no one is close enough to hear it, how much of an asshole is Ladd? Perhaps not the most elegantly presented philosophical riddle, but you get my point. Privacy meant Ladd could be doing anything out here. Anything he wanted.

I continued up the hill, checking the addresses. Ladd's house was coming up, just around the bend. I think I was holding my breath.

The curve in the road came and went, and there, appearing at the far end of a sweeping driveway, was Ladd's sprawling home, a home that could have doubled as a compound for a Colombian drug lord.

I drove slowly past it, giving it only a casual glance, and immediately two things caught my eye. One, there appeared to be a guest house behind the main home. Two—and this was a big two—a white cargo van was parked in the driveway. I didn't see Ladd's Benz, but it could have been parked inside the garage.

As I continued past, I noted the front yard of the property was not gated, and the house itself appeared oddly empty and devoid of life, but that was only my gut reaction to the place.

I continued past it and parked in a sort of dirt cul-de-sac at the top of the street. A handful of other cars were already parked here, and the cul-de-sac, I recalled, was actually the launching point to a fairly popular hiking trail down into the canyon. A trail that led away from Ladd's home. The parked cars were a blessing. Now I could hunker down without drawing attention to myself.

Good for me.

I backed into an spot, and from this vantage point, I could look down onto many of the homes on the street below. But not Ladd's. It was still hidden behind a dense thicket of trees and bushes.

Damn.

Laurel Canyon is comprised of a lot of hills, valleys and glens. This past winter had been a particularly wet one, and everything was still brightly green and verdant. That would all change once summer hit. Through my windshield, I watched a brown hawk slowly circle the sky. Somewhere out there something small and furry didn't stand a chance.

I continued sitting there in the driver's seat, drumming my fingers on the steering wheel, wondering what the hell to do next.

The hawk continued circling. The sun continued setting. I was parked directly above Ladd's spacious home, but I couldn't see into it, although I had a hell of a clear shot of the main house's roof and guest house's roof.

Must be nice.

Of course, this coming from a guy who once owned something called Graceland. Another life, another time.

Another *lifetime.*

The hawk suddenly swooped low and hard, and disappeared behind a copse of trees. A heartbeat or two later, it appeared again, this time with something small dangling from its talons. I think it was a cottontail. Poor Peter. The hawk and its dinner rose higher and higher, then banked to port and was gone.

So what now?

Plan B.

And what was plan B?

I didn't know, but I sure as hell better figure it out quick. Now, if I couldn't watch the house from the front, or from above, there was always the *back*, right? And, from where I sat, I could see the back of his house consisted of nothing but wooded wilderness.

Good for me. I think.

With Plan B taking shape, I stepped out of my car and went around to the trunk. There, I found a pair of binoculars and Mace in my emergency kit. I slipped the Mace into my front pocket, strapped the high-powered binoculars around my neck, and wondered what exactly I was doing.

Plan B, of course.

Oh, yeah. That.

Off to the side of the dirt road was the popular hiking trail that led down into the canyon. I said a little prayer, and then started down the trail.

CHAPTER FIFTY-SIX

The trail was actually wide enough to be called a small road. *Not exactly roughing it out here.* I was willing to bet a convenient doggie-poopie bag dispenser or two would be set up somewhere along the path, complete with convenient drinking fountains and bathrooms for the humans.

Maybe even an espresso stand.

I hadn't planned on a hike today. Admittedly, I also hadn't planned on coming across my number-one suspect. These things happen. You adapt, roll with it. Luckily, I had been dressed in my all-purpose crime-fighting gear. Superman has his blue tights. I had my blue jeans, sneakers and polo shirt.

Good 'nuff.

The sun was setting beyond the western foothills, and the sky was awash in pale yellows, oranges and reds. The air was filled with a heady mix of sage and juniper, and a dozen or so other scents that my uninitiated nose couldn't distinguish.

Scrubby trees crowded the trail. The occasional beaver tail cacti was mixed with barrel cacti and other succulents that I couldn't name, either. Maybe I should invest in a *Peterson's Field Guide to Southern California Flora and Fauna.*

Or not.

Other than the little critters that scurried off into the brush—mostly lizards, no doubt—I was alone on the trail. The hikers were no doubt much further along, or busy in the many port-a-potties.

Five minutes or so into my hike, I was already dripping sweat and wishing I had brought a bottle of water. No doubt all those damned Frappuccinos had seriously dehydrated me. And just as I was wondering if these barrel cactus had any water in them, I came across a water fountain. Nice. Next to the fountain was a bowl for your dog, and next to the bowl was a blue plastic crate with a recycling sticker on it. The plastic crate was nearly full with empty water bottles and other plastic bottles filled with the latest, high-tech water. I wondered if they were going to recycle the plastic crate, too. Anyway, still grateful—and maybe a little cranky from the heat—I drank deeply from the water fountain.

When I finally pulled away from the life-giving, stainless steel teat, water dribbling from my chin and down the front of my shirt, I took stock of my present location. To my right was some rather dense woodland, a rarity here in southern California. To my left, about a mile or so away, were the houses, including Ladd's spacious estate. Straight ahead, the path continued down into the canyon, curving gently away from civilization.

Time to rough it.

I stepped off the main dirt path, stepped over knee-high grass and weeds, pushed aside a pathetic young scrub tree, and blazed my own trail.

The setting sun still had some heat. Sweat was still on my brow and presently streaming down the center of my back. And, of course, the instant I had stepped off the main trail, a spur of some sort had worked its way deep into my shoe. As I paused to dig it free, dozens of pesky gnats appeared as if from nowhere, circling my head like so many satellites.

I wanted a beer. *Bad.*

I waved them away and set out on a course that would, ideally, lead me directly behind Ladd's home. The closer I got to the homes, the quieter I tried to be, but I think I probably still sounded like a bear drunk on fermented elderberries.

Davy Crockett I'm not.

And soon, slightly out of breath and thinking that a cane about now would have been a hell of a good idea, I came up behind Ladd's sweeping home.

And directly in front of me was the guest house, where a light was on inside.

It appears Ladd had a guest.

CHAPTER FIFTY-SEVEN

Admittedly, I had never done surveillance *behind* a house before, and probably never would again. Hey, life is full of firsts. At least, back here in the woods, there weren't any nosy neighbors to contend with. Coyote poo, yes. Rattlesnakes, yes. Nosy Nellies, no.

So far, other than the swarming gnats, which, I think, thought of me as their mother ship, nature was keeping herself at bay. Which was a very, very good thing.

I positioned myself on a grassy knoll above the northwest section of the house. From here I had a fine view into the backyard. A six-foot, stone fence encircled the entire back lot.

I figured I might be here a while. Hell, I might here all night, which had me wondering what sort of man-eaters roamed these hills in the dark? Mountain lions? Coyotes? Sasquatches?

So I hunkered down and took stock of the surrounding bushes and trees, feeling confident that I couldn't be spotted by anyone inside Ladd's house. Granted, a hungry mountain lion with a hankering for hound dog could be a problem.

And, yeah, I'm all hound dog, baby.

From my perch on the knoll, I lifted my binoculars and slowly scanned Ladd's backyard. Ah, there was an inviting-looking pool and an equally inviting-looking Jacuzzi. A brick outdoor grill, two patio tables with blue umbrellas. The backyard was mostly paved, but there were small patches of grass here and there. An actual dog house was sitting on one of those grassy patches. A *big* dog house. Damn. Scattered throughout the grass like steaming land mines were so many dog piles. *Big* dog piles.

So far there wasn't any sign of the dog, although I seriously doubted this dog would turn out to be fake. Maybe it was inside with Ladd, or snoozing inside it's spacious dog house.

The main house was a single-story ranch with clapboards and vertical siding, concrete chimney and wood shingled roof. There was even an iron weather vane rooster on one of the cupolas. For someone I seriously suspected of having abducted another human being, Ladd was surprisingly exhibitionistic, as most of the curtains and blinds were wide open. Perhaps he never suspected someone would approach from the rear of the house. Perhaps he liked living dangerously. Or perhaps I was barking up the wrong tree.

A coyote howled from somewhere.

Bad choice of words. I suddenly felt very alone and very exposed out in the woodland. Granted, this wasn't the deep, dark woods, but I was an old man with old knees, surrounded by hungry coyotes.

Don't be such a baby.

Something scurried in the brush next to me, and I jumped like a schoolgirl. I whipped around in time to see a squirrel scurry up the twisted trunk of an ancient, dusty-looking tree.

Relax. Deep breaths.

I turned back to the gated home before me. I knew Ladd was my guy, and I knew this to the very core of my being. Call it a gut feeling. Call it instinct. Call it whatever you want. Either way, he was dirty.

The house was silent. The only indication that someone might be inside was an ambient, bluish glow coming from deep within the house. Then again, it could have been anything. Glow from a computer screen. Night Light. Portal into Hell. And with the dwindling daylight, the hint of light was turning into something more than a hint. My best guess was that Ladd was alone and watching TV.

I turned the field glasses over to the guest house.

It was a mini-ranch house, complete with pitched roof and clapboards and a brick veneer. It was quite a bit smaller than the main house, but still bigger than my apartment. Suddenly depressed, I slid the binoculars over to a pair of double windows facing me on the west side of the house.

And froze.

There was a face in the window, watching me. And not just any face.

It was Miranda Scott.

CHAPTER FIFTY-EIGHT

I blinked and gasped and the face in the window was instantly gone, replaced now by swaying dark curtains. I lowered the field glasses.

What the hell had I just seen?

Surely I was hallucinating. I mean, c'mon, I'd been obsess-ing over Miranda's face for two weeks now. This was a classic case of wish-fulfillment. I *wanted* to find her, and so I did. At least in my mind. The face had probably belonged to someone else, and I had transposed it with Miranda's own. That is, if the face was even there to start with. Maybe I had made it up.

Great theory. Now convince your hammering heart.

I lifted the field glasses again, but now the curtains hung limply, inertly. They completely concealed the window.

It had been her. It had been her. And she had been watching me.

I took a deep, shuddering breath. I had just exhaled when the rear sliding glass door to the main house opened. I swung the binoculars to the left and watched as Gregory Ladd appeared, wearing a silk Oriental robe and holding a bottle of wine and a single wine glass. Almost immediately a rottweiler—and easily one of the biggest dogs I'd ever seen—appeared by his side. Ladd promptly kicked it away, cursing at it. The dog yelped and skittered away, although it was too big to skitter very far. It came back for more but kept its distance, its nub of a tail wagging, looking confused but in need of attention. It got none from Ladd, who instead headed straight for the guest house. He crossed the small area between the main house and the guest house, an area about the width of his pool, and then disappeared around the corner of the guest house. A few seconds later I heard a door open, then slam shut.

A light turned on in the guest house.

* * *

My chest hurt. The hike down the trail, although not particularly strenuous, had taken a lot out of me. I forced myself to take deep breaths.

If that had indeed been Miranda, then what the hell was going on inside there? If she was indeed trapped, why not just bust out the window and get the hell out of there? Obviously, she wasn't being restrained. Was she in there on her own free will? I didn't know, but she could explain it to the cops.

Yes, the cops!

I pulled my cell phone, flipped it open. No reception. Should have known. Never once, ever, had I gotten reception out here in the past.

No problem, right? Just hike back out of here, find my car, drive around until I get cell reception, and then make the call to Detective Colbert.

Good enough.

And just as I turned to head back up the trail, I heard something that chilled me to my very core. An ear-splitting scream, and it came from the guest house.

CHAPTER FIFTY-NINE

I stopped in my tracks and turned back to the guest house, torn about what I should do. Stay or go for help? And if I stayed, what the hell could I possibly do? I was an old man with a can of Mace. Ladd was huge—and he had a rottweiler, to boot.

And as I stood there, debating what to do, another scream ripped through the dusk air.

And another.

And another.

Jesus! My blood ran cold. The rottweiler, which had been pacing out in front of the small house, paused, lifted its ears, and then resumed its pacing. Perhaps it was used to the screaming.

I wasn't.

Another scream. This one more blood curdling than the others. The screams, although loud to me due to my proximity, were still oddly muffled, as if the house had been sound proofed.

What the fuck is going on in there?

The scream came again, this time long and wavering and filled with hysteria and pain and fear, and no one heard it.

No one but me.

I removed the Mace from my pocket, gripped it firmly. There was no time for the police. I dashed toward the guest house, realizing that a gun about now would have been nice. *Too late now.*

I reached the outer stone fence. The rottweiler, perhaps agitated and distracted by the screaming coming from within the guest house, hadn't noticed me yet. I didn't blame it. Hell, I was agitated and distracted by the screaming.

I knew I had to act, and I knew I had to act *now*. I also knew that I was about to confront one hell of a big dog, and all I had for protection was an aerosol spray can.

Fuck me.

Just as I reached the outer stone fence, sucking wind, another scream, much louder and more prolonged than the others, pierced the cooling late afternoon air. Maybe it just seemed louder than the others because I was closer to the guest house now. Maybe. Either way, it raised the hair on my neck.

I'm Elvis fucking Presley. I used to sing in the Astrodome. I used to make movies. The world adores me to this day, and probably forever will. So what the hell am I doing out here?

Good question. Night was falling rapidly. A cool wind made its way around the house, lifting my dyed brown hair. Sweat stung my eyes.

Deep breaths, big guy. You can do this.

Another scream, followed now by a lot of whimpering. I checked my cell phone, still no signal.

It looks like it's just you and your can of Mace, big guy.

I'm a lover, not a fighter, although, as an actor, I had been trained to punch, or at least to *simulate* a punch. In real life, I rarely, if ever, got into brawls.

I'm too old for brawls. I'm too pretty for brawls.

The Mace did not feel reassuring. It felt small and inadequate and I could almost feel the dog's teeth sinking into my calf now.

Fuck.

Deep breaths.

Another, piercing scream. My blood ran cold. Hell, my blood felt as it had frozen in my veins.

Do it. Now!

I reached for the top of the stone fence and started climbing.

CHAPTER SIXTY

Up I went, clambering awkwardly, banging my old knees, scratching my old forearms. I hadn't climbed an eight-foot fence in God knows how long, maybe since I was a kid, and the can of Mace in my hand made climbing especially cumbersome.

Grunting and nearly falling backwards, I finally swung a leg up and over the top of the fence. From that position, with one leg hanging over each side, gasping for breath, I looked into Ladd's backyard—and my heart stopped cold.

The rottweiler was no longer distracted by the screaming from the guest house. No, it was focused on something else entirely. *Me.* It stood about thirty feet away, frozen in mid-pace, staring at me, drool oozing from its hanging jowls.

We stared at each other for another second or two.

And then it charged, hitting top speed in two strides or less. The deepest, most horrific growl I had ever heard in my life erupted from its massive lungs.

I dropped down from the wall—and promptly landed on the edge of something, perhaps a rock or a brick. Either way, my ankle rolled, something snapped, and I cried out. Searing, white-hot pain lanced through me. I collapsed in the surrounding weeds, and lost the can of Mace in the process.

From my side, I had a ground's-eye view of the charging rottweiler, and it wasn't a pretty sight. All teeth and slobber and muscle and jawbone. The ground actually shook. My bowels instantly turned to water.

Gasping, I groped frantically for the Mace, searching the weeds and grass.

The dog continued to charge.

My fingertips touched something metal and round.

The dog lunged.

I threw myself back against the stone wall and swung my hand around and pressed the dispenser as hard as I could, praying to sweet Jesus that the nozzle was facing *away* from me—

A powerful jet of oleo-resin capsicum erupted from the canister and straight into the charging dog's face. The rottweiler reacted instantly. It lost its footing, tumbled, and slammed sideways into me. Then it proceeded to claw at its face with both paws, backing away and yelping loudly and continuously. A hideous, pitiful sound.

It backed all the way onto the brick path that ran around the perimeter of the backyard. Once on the path, the dog, amazingly, began running. And it ran blind, banging its way around the side of the guest house and disappearing from view, where it crashed loudly into what I assumed was some sort of metal trash can. Probably put a hell of a dent in the can.

And loud enough to wake the dead.

I had to hurry. Ignoring the pain in my right ankle, I used the wall to help me find my feet, and then hopped on one foot over to the side of the guest house. My ankle was bad. Very bad. I leaned against the corner of the house, sucking air, sick to my stomach.

A door opened slowly from around the corner.

I fought to control my breathing. The dog was still making hideous noises from the rear of the guest house. I felt bad for it, even though it would have surely ripped my throat out. And I needed that throat. I had my first gig on Monday, which I fully intended to make.

"Purgatory?" said a voice hesitantly. It was Ladd's voice. It came again: "Purgie?"

Purgie?

The dog didn't respond, although it did howl even louder.

"I've got a gun," said Ladd loudly. I assumed he wasn't talking to Purgie.

Now I heard footsteps. Ladd was trying to be quiet but I heard him crunching carefully over some loose rocks. Behind me, Purgie had settled down a little, although he/she/it was still whimpering pitifully.

Another crunch. Closer now.

I gripped the Mace, making sure it was faced away from me. I raised it up, and waited.

CHAPTER SIXTY-ONE

I held my breath.

From within the guest house came the sounds of someone sobbing. A *woman* sobbing. And from around the corner from where I was standing, I could hear someone breathing. Ragged breathing. Nervous breathing. Scared breathing.

I gripped the Mace. *Lord help me.*

I wasn't even entirely sure of the Mace's range. Something like that might have been a good thing to know.

Too late to worry about it now.

I took a deep breath, held it. More ragged breathing from around the corner. More scraping footsteps. And now I could smell faint traces of alcohol. And sweat. Lots of sweat, and it wasn't my own.

I remembered his words: *"I have a gun."*

I still had the element of surprise, which meant I had to move *now.* But I didn't want to move now. The guy around the corner had a fucking gun, and all I had was a fucking little can of Mace, which might as well have been a can of spray deodorant.

But I had the element of surprise. And the Mace wasn't deodorant. I had seen the effect it had had on the rottweiler.

Just get him straight in the face, King. The eyes. And don't expose your body.

When I saw the barefoot appear from around the corner, I dropped to a knee, swung my arm around the corner, and fired the Mace.

Ladd was there, completely naked, holding a hunting rifle. He had also been looking to his right, which was good for me. By the time his peripheral vision caught movement to his left, the Mace had already hit him straight in the face. Granted, my first shot hit him somewhere in his disgusting, jiggling torso, but I moved the powerful stream up and into his face.

He swung his weapon around, but it was too late. Screaming, he flung the rifle aside and clawed at his eyes like a wild animal, cursing and spitting. I stood and moved around the corner and kept on spraying him until he lay curled on the ground, whimpering and moaning.

And even then, I continued spraying until the canister was empty.

CHAPTER SIXTY-TWO

Hopping on one foot and dragging the other, I retrieved Ladd's rifle. With the producer currently incapacitated and whimpering feebly—and the dog nowhere to be found—I headed over to the guest house. I actually used the rifle as a cane. Once at the door, I paused to gather what little wits I had remaining, and tried the handle. Locked, of course. The keys were with Ladd, perhaps still clutched in his hands, but he was currently writhing and thrashing and not being very accommodating.

Sobbing from within the guest house.

Lord, Jesus.

Maybe if I had two good legs I could have kicked the door in. *Or tried to.* Instead, I found a fist-sized rock in a nearby flower garden, and proceeded to bash the doorknob until the fucking thing fell off, making enough racket to wake the dead. I didn't care about the dead. I cared about the person crying within.

Blood pounding in my ears, adrenalin surging through my veins, I pushed the badly damaged door open, and stepped inside, holding the rifle out before me.

"Hello," I said.

I was greeted by an overwhelming stench. No, nothing rotting. Just filthy human waste. Sweat and excrement and piss and anything else that could come from a human body. Bile rose sharply in the back of my throat, but I held it together. I stepped deeper into the room, holding the rifle out before me like a bayonet.

"Hello," I called again. "I saw you earlier, looking at me through the window."

No response, although I heard something close to whimpering now coming from down a small hallway. The guest house was probably one bedroom, one bathroom. I was currently standing in a small, dark living room. The room was decorated modestly with a couch, love seat and reading chair, but I had a sense that it wasn't used much.

I crossed through the room and headed slowly down the short hallway. The whimpering was growing louder. The stench was growing stronger, too. I fought to control the gorge rising up in my throat.

There was a light on in the room at the end of the hallway. Along the way, I took a peek inside a small and disgusting-looking bathroom. Towels and clothing were every where. So was fecal matter, as if whoever had tried to use the bathroom had no clue what to do or how to do it.

My stomach heaved. I fought through it.

I came up to the bedroom. The door was cracked open. Yellow light issued out. Anything could be beyond that door. Anything at all. How do you prepare yourself for the unexpected.

You don't. You can't.

I pushed the door open with the tip of the rifle. The room was small, made smaller by a massive four-poster bed sitting squarely in the center of the room. Leather straps hung from the bed's crossbeams. Next to the bed, close to the door, was a low bookcase. Lining the top shelf were whips and chains, ball gags, dildos, anal plugs, and every other type of kinky toy known to man.

On the corner of the bookcase was a small pile of pills—roofies, no doubt. Ladd had probably kept her drugged and high for the past two weeks.

Speaking of *her*, in the center of the bed, partially hidden by what could only be described as a very disgusting comforter, was a human figure. A lithe figure who was crying softly.

I stepped deeper into the room, confident that there was no one else in here. I moved over to the bed, reached down, and pulled up one corner of the comforter. There, shaking badly, naked and curled in the fetal position, covered in cuts and bruises and sweat and tears and stink, was Hollywood's newest starlet, Miranda Scott.

I covered her back up and used the phone in the guest house to call Detective Colbert.

CHAPTER SIXTY-THREE

I stood with Detective Colbert in Ladd's spacious kitchen. We were alone, looking out through the sliding glass door. The sky beyond the distant rolling hills was purple and eternal. Less eternal, and a lot closer, the guest house was a beehive of activity as crime scene investigators did their thing. Earlier, with sirens blaring and lights flashing, Miranda had been rushed off to a nearby hospital. All indications were that she was going to be fine, at least physically.

Colbert said, "The screaming you heard. We figure she was having a bad trip. There weren't any fresh wounds. At least, none that we could see initially. Probably gave her too much of something, or gave her something she couldn't handle. Either way, she isn't coherent right now, so we don't know the full extent of what he's done to her."

"But she's alive," I said.

"Yes," he said.

"You think he was going to kill her?"

"Hard to say. We'll go through the place thoroughly. But so far, looks like he kept her here for his own sick pleasure." Colbert still wouldn't look at me. Jaw rigid, he kept his gaze on the guest house outside. "I've got more news."

"Go on."

"Dana Scott confessed to killing Flip Barowski."

I nodded. We both looked out through the glass door. The early night sky was now mostly black now, with a smattering of stars. If not for the L.A. smog there would have been more than just a smattering of stars.

Colbert continued, "I approached Dana myself, asked her what she knew about the killing, and she broke down instantly. Told me everything. She has a pistol at home, owned by her deceased husband. She calls the kid up and tells him she hears that he's seeing her daughter again. He says yes, and she tells him to stay away from her daughter. He says no, that he loves her. She says fine, let's talk about it, and he agrees. They were supposed to meet in a parking lot, but she comes up behind him and puts a bullet in his head."

"Just like she promised she would do," I said.

"Okay, fine. I get that. The mother warned the kid to stay away, and he doesn't stay away. That doesn't explain how Miranda ends up here, in this sicko's house, being sexually abused for the last two weeks."

"I think he was following her," I said.

"Then kidnaps her? Not even your bum claims he heard her resisting."

"I say he approached her in the van as she came out of the store. Made it seem like a coincidence. Probably offered to buy her dinner. Maybe talk about a movie deal."

"Not to mention her boyfriend had just been murdered," said Colbert. "Maybe she was looking for a friend to talk to."

"So he entices her inside his van. She has no problem getting inside, thinking of him as a friend, an ex-boss, the person who gave her her first big break."

"So she gets in the van...." added Colbert.

"And he takes her back to his place. Maybe offers her a drink—"

"And the sick fuck slips her a roofie," said Colbert.

"That's the way I see it," I said.

"Well, we'll know more when she comes down from her high. Luckily nothing appears to be permanent. Physically, she'll come out of this fine. Emotionally...."

"Emotionally, she's going to need a lifetime of therapy."

We were silent, contemplative. I had taken some pain killers that I found in Ladd's cupboards. The pain in my ankle was still there, but it had been reduced to a dull throbbing. I can handle a dull throbbing.

I'll take some Vicodins later. Knock it right out.

I said, "Some people obsessed over her, sometimes even for years. Some people just followed her around like lovestruck puppies."

"And this sick fucker takes it a step further."

"Yes," I said.

We were silent some more. The purple was gone from the sky, and more stars came out. The crime scene crew was still going in and out of the guest house. I wondered if Ladd had any buried bodies out here, or if this had been a one-time thing? Hard to say, but I suspected Ladd had been obsessing about her for years. Much like Flip Barowski. And perhaps many other males Miranda came into contact with.

"You found her, King," said Colbert.

"Not bad for an old man," I said.

"Not bad for anyone."

CHAPTER SIXTY-FOUR

The lights were bright, just the way I remembered them. The Pussycat was packed, just the way I remembered most of my concerts. The crowd was older, which was fine. So was I.

Seated in the back, behind the dance floor at a small round table, were four people. My personal guests for the night. Clarke was there, nearly drunk. I could just make him out. He hadn't taken his eyes off me all night long. Kelly my on again/off again was seated next to him. She looked elegant and sophisticated and damn beautiful. I also noticed she had accepted a drink or two from some other men, talking to them, laughing with them, touching them, flirting with them. Sigh. It's hell being in an open relationship, but there you have it. The gal sitting next to her often had my full and undivided attention. My therapist, Dr. Vivian. She kept her eyes on me and ignored the attention of the other men. I loved that about her. The last guest was, of course, Miranda. The young starlet looked beautiful and captivating, easily the most beautiful girl here tonight. Everyone knew it. But she seemed impervious to the attention, completely unaware. She also looked dead, lifeless, although once or twice I had caught her tapping her fingers and bobbing her head to the music. She was coming around, slowly, but the healing process would take a lifetime, if ever.

I had spent the weekend alone, trying to sober up. Now I was down to just five Vicodins a day, but I wanted more. Many more. It was a start.

Becky and I worked well together. Smooth transitions from one song to the next. She was a talented pianist, versatile, and I am an old pro, although a little rusty.

As I sang, as I did my groovy thing, I noticed a crowd was gathering at the nightclub's main entrance. Someone was there. Someone important, obviously.

I used to be important. Maybe someday I would be again. Maybe. But then again, I had given all this up before. Did I really want it all back again?

Maybe. Maybe not.

Anyway, whoever was causing the commotion was now making their way towards the stage area, towards me. The crowd was following, forming and reforming, a sort of moving huddle. I kept singing, but I also kept my eye on whoever was approaching.

And when the crowd finally parted, when I saw for the first time who was causing all the ruckus, I gasped.

It's nearly impossible for me to be star-struck, but I was this evening. It was the brightest star of them all.

My baby girl Lisa took a seat in a booth against the far wall, surrounded by a small entourage of men and women and bodyguards. She signed a dozen or so autographs before her bodyguards closed in around her. Most in the crowd got the hint and dispersed, although some still buzzed around her.

I stopped singing. Hell, I *couldn't* sing. Becky glanced over at me from the piano, eyebrows raised. I quickly gave her the thumbs up. She shrugged and went on playing.

And when I looked back at my daughter's table, I saw her looking at me. No, *staring* at me. My breath caught. I think her breath caught, too. And then, slowly, slowly she smiled. A big, beautiful smile.

Did she know who I was? I think so. Recognition seemed to have dawned across her face. Perhaps she had known who I was before coming, and so the shock to her wasn't so great.

I didn't know, but I did know one thing: someone had set this all up. Someone who had known about her and me. Someone who had known where I lived. The anonymous watch. The CDs. The CDs that weren't even available on the market yet. CDs that were privy to only a select few, including entertainment attorneys.

I finally put it all together.

I looked at Clarke. He was grinning like a schoolboy, or a drunkard. He winked at me, looking pleased as hell. I would kill him later.

No, I'm going to kiss him later.

I found my voice again, which came stronger and clearer. Becky nodded at me and continued hitting the keys and doing her groovy thing, and when the song was over, I spoke into the microphone.

"Ladies and gentleman, we have a special guest here tonight." Most in the crowd stopped dancing or looked up from their tables. I continued, "She's a beautiful little thing who makes her daddy so proud." I sounded like Elvis. I knew it, but didn't give a damn. "Lisa Marie Presley, ladies and gentleman."

I pointed to her, and the crowd turned—especially those who were unaware of her entrance—and a massive cheer erupted. From her seat, she blushed mightily and waved, but never once did she take her eyes off me.

"Come up here, little lady, and sing a song with me."

She didn't budge. Not at first. The crowd cheered louder and urged her onward. She finally gave in, as I knew she would. She slipped out of the booth, smiling shyly.

With a bodyguard trailing behind, she made her way up to the stage. The big guy held out a hand and she used it to step up onto the stage. The crowd cheered harder.

She ignored them all and kept her eyes on me.

I ignored them, too, and held out my own hand. She crossed the stage and stepped into the light and she was the most beautiful thing I had ever seen in my life. She took my hand, and I pulled her into me, as if we were dancing. There were tears in her eyes and I think she was shaking.

"Daddy?" she asked me, although I could barely hear her words. Mostly I read her lips, and, I'm sure, others did as well.

"It's me, little darlin'."

I looked over at Becky, whose mouth was hanging open. I motioned for her to play something, and she finally did, something by Elvis. "Love Me Tender."

Bill the manager with his blue shades came running out on stage. He placed an extra mic in front of my daughter, sneaking a peak at the two of us together, shock on his face. He quickly dashed off the stage. Those on the dance floor had quit dancing. Those drinking beer had quit drinking beer. A very surreal quiet descended over the Pussycat. I sensed all eyes on us, and I sensed many open mouths. And then I heard the whisperings of "Elvis." And then the whisperings grew louder and louder, until they were chanting my name.

"Are you ready, baby?" I asked her.

"I'm ready, daddy."

"Follow my lead," I said. "Like old times."

"Like old times," she said.

The End

Also available:

TEMPLE OF THE JAGUAR

Nick Caine Series #1
by J.R. Rain and Aiden James
A lost city.
A beautiful archaeologist.
And one antiquities thief who is in way over his head.

Available now!
Kindle * Kobo * Nook
Amazon UK * Apple * Smashwords
Paperback * Audio Book

JUDAS SILVER: AN ADVENTURE NOVEL

by J.R. Rain and Elizabeth Basque
Thirty cursed coins.
A plot to unleash hell on earth.
And one relic hunter who's in way over his head.

Available now!
Amazon * Kobo * Nook
Amazon UK * Apple * Smashwords
Paperback * Audio Book

THE LOST ARK
by J.R. Rain
A missing professor.
A mysterious map.
The archaeological discovery of a lifetime.

Available now!
Kindle * Kobo * Nook
Amazon UK * Apple * Smashwords
Paperback * Audio Book

Also available :

DARK HORSE
A Jim Knighthorse Novel
by J.R. Rain

Dark Horse is available at:
Kindle * Kobo * Nook
Amazon UK * Apple * Smashwords
Paperback * Audio Book

CHAPTER ONE

Charles Brown, the defense attorney, was a small man with a round head. He was wearing a brown and orange zigzagged power tie. I secretly wondered if he went by Charlie as a kid and had a dog named Snoopy and a crush on the little red-headed girl.

We were sitting in my office on a warm spring day. Charlie was here to give me a job if I wanted it, and I wanted it. I hadn't worked in two weeks and was beginning to like it, which made me nervous.

"I think the kid's innocent," he was saying.

"Of course you do, Charlie. You're a defense attorney. You would find cause to think Jack the Ripper was simply a misunderstood artist before his time."

He looked at me with what was supposed to be a stern face.

"The name's Charles," he said.

"If you say so."

"I do."

"Glad that's cleared up."

"I heard you could be difficult," he said. "Is this you being difficult? If so, then I'm disappointed."

I smiled. "Maybe you have me confused with my father."

Charlie sat back in my client chair and smiled. His domed head was perfectly buffed and polished, cleanly reflecting the halogen lighting above. His skin appeared wet and viscous, as if his sweat glands were ready to spring into action at a moment's notice.

"Your father has quite a reputation in L.A. I gave his office a call before coming here. Of course, he's quite busy and could not take on an extra case."

"So you settled on the next best thing."

"If you want to call it that," he said. "I've heard that you've performed adequately with similar cases, and so I've decided to give you a shot, although my expectations are not very high, and I have another P.I. waiting in the wings."

"How reassuring," I said.

"Yeah, well, he's established. You're not."

"But can he pick up a blind side blitz?"

Charlie smiled and splayed his stubby fingers flat on my desk and looked around my office, which was adorned with newspaper clippings and photographs of yours truly. Most of the photographs depict me in a Bruin uniform, sporting the number 45. In most I'm carrying the football, and in others I'm blowing open the hole for the tailback. Or at least I like to think I'm blowing open the hole. The newspapers are yellowing now, taped or tacked to the wood paneling. Maybe someday I'll take them down. But not yet.

"You beat SC a few years back. I can never forgive you for that. Two touchdowns in the fourth quarter alone."

"Three," I said. "But who's counting?"

He rubbed his chin. "Destroyed your leg, if I recall, in the last game of the season. Broken in seven different places."

"Nine, but who's counting?"

"Must have been hard to deal with. You were on your way to the pros. Would have made a hell of a fullback."

That *had* been hard to deal with, and I didn't feel like talking about it now to Charlie Brown. "Why do you believe in your client's innocence?" I asked.

He looked at me. "I see. You don't want to talk about it. Sorry I brought it up." He crossed his legs. He didn't seem sorry at all. He looked smugly down at his shoes, which had polish on the polish. "Because I believe Derrick's story. I believe he loved his girlfriend and would never kill her."

"People have been killed for love before. Nothing new."

On my computer screen before me I had brought up an article from the Orange County Register. The article showed a black teen being led away into a police car. He was looking down, his head partially covered by his jacket. He was being led away from a local high school. A very upscale high school, if I recalled. The story was dated three weeks ago, and I recalled reading it back then.

I tapped the computer monitor. "The police say there's some indication that his girlfriend was seeing someone else, and that jealousy might have been a factor."

"Yes," said the attorney. "And we think this someone else framed our client."

"I take it you want me to find this man."

"Or person."

"Ah, equality," I said.

"We want you to find evidence of our client's innocence, whether or not you find the true murderer."

"Anything else I should know?"

"We feel race might be a factor here. He was the only black student in school, and in the neighborhood."

"I believe the preferred term is African-American."

"I'm aware of public sentiment in this regards. I don't need you to lecture me."

"Just trying to live up to my difficult name."

"Yeah, well, cool it," he said. "Now, no one's talking at the school. My client says he was working out late in the school gym, yet no one saw him, not even the janitors."

"Then maybe he wasn't there."

"He was there," said Charlie simply, as if his word was enough. "So do you want the job?"

"Sure."

We discussed a retainer fee and then he wrote me a check. When he left, waddling out of the office, I could almost hear Schroeder playing on his little piano in the background.

CHAPTER TWO

"He was found with the murder weapon," said Detective Hanson. "It was in the backseat of his car. That's damning evidence."

"That," I said, "and he's black."

"And he's black," said Hanson.

"In an all white school," I said.

"Yep."

"Were his prints on the knife?"

"No."

We were sitting in an outdoor café facing the beach. It was spring, and in southern California that's as good as summer. Many underdressed women were roller-blading, jogging or walking their dogs on the narrow beach path. There were also some men, all finely chiseled, but they were not as interesting.

Detective Hanson was a big man, but not as big as me. He had neat brown hair parted down the middle. His thick mustache screamed cop. He wore slacks and a white shirt. He was sweating through his shirt. I was dressed in khaki shorts, a surfing T-shirt and white Vans. Coupled with my amazing tan and disarming smile, I was surprised I wasn't more often confused with Jimmy Buffet. If Jimmy Buffet stood six foot four and weighed two hundred and twenty.

"You guys have anything else on the kid?" I asked.

"You know I can't divulge that. Trial hasn't even started. The info about the knife made it to the press long ago, so that's a freebie for you. I can tell you this: the body was found at one a.m., although the ME places the time of death around seven p.m. the previous night."

"Who found the body?"

"A neighbor."

"Where were the victim's parents?"

"Dinner and dancing. It was a Friday night."

"Of course," I said. "Who doesn't go out and dance on a Friday night?"

"I don't," said Hanson.

"Me neither," I said. "Does Derrick have an alibi?"

"This will cost you a tunacoda."

"You drive a hard bargain."

I called the waitress over and put in our lunch orders.

"No alibi," Hanson said when she had left, "but...." He let his voice trail off.

"But you believe the kid?"

He shrugged. "Yeah. He seems like a good kid. Says he was working out at the school gym at the time."

"Schools have janitors, staff, students."

"Yeah, well, it was late and no one saw him."

"Or no one chose to see him."

Hanson shrugged.

Our food arrived. A tunacoda for the detective. A half pound burger for me, with grilled onions and cheese, and a milkshake.

"You trying to commit suicide?" he asked.

"I'm bulking up," I said.

"This is how you bulk up? Eating crap?"

"Only way I know how."

"Why?"

"Thinking of trying out for San Diego," I said.

"The Chargers?"

"Yeah."

"What about your leg?"

"The leg's going to be a problem."

He thought about that, working his way through his tuna and avocado sandwich. He took a sip from his Coke.

"You wanna bash heads with other men and snap each other in the shower with jock straps, go right ahead."

"It's not as glamorous as that."

"Suicide, I say. What's your dad think?"

"He doesn't know. You're the first person I've told."

"I'm honored."

"You should be."

"What's Cindy going to say?"

I sipped my milkshake. "She won't like it, but she will support me. She happens to think very highly of me and my decisions."

He snorted and finished his sandwich, grabbed his Styrofoam cup.

"I can't believe I was bribed with a shitty tuna sandwich and a Coke."

"A simple man with simple needs."

"I should resent that remark, if it wasn't so true." He stood. "I gotta run. Good luck with the kid, but I think it's a lost cause. Kid even has a record."

"What kind?"

"Vandalism, mostly. He's a goner. Hear they're gonna try him as an adult."

Detective Hanson left with his Styrofoam cup. I noticed he wasn't wearing socks. Even cops in Huntington Beach are cool.

CHAPTER THREE

Cindy Darwin is an anthropology professor at UCI. Her expertise is in the anthropology of religion, which, she tells me, is an important aspect of anthropology. And, yes, she can trace her lineage back to Charles Darwin, which makes her a sort of icon in her field. She knows more things about anthropology than she probably should, and too few things about the real world. Maybe that's why she keeps me around.

It was late and we were walking hand-in-hand along the Huntington Pier. From here we could see the lights of Catalina Island, where the reclusive sorts live and travel via ferry and plane. To the north, in the far distance, we could see Long Beach glittering away. The air was cool and windy and we were dressed in light jackets and jeans. Her jeans were much snugger and more form-fitting than mine. As they should be.

"I'm thinking of giving San Diego a call," I said.

"Who's in San Diego?" she asked. She had a slightly higher pitched voice than most women. I found it endlessly sexy. She said her voice made it easier to holler across an assembly hall. Gave it more range, or something.

I was silent. She put two and two together. She let go of my hand.

"They call you again?" she asked. "The Rams, right?"

"The Chargers. Christ, Cindy, your own brother plays on the team."

"I think it's all sort of silly. Football, I mean. And all those silly mascots, I just don't get it."

"The mascots help us boys tell the teams apart," I said. "And, no, they didn't call. But I'm thinking about their last offer."

"Honey, that was two years ago."

She was right. I turned them down two years ago. My leg hadn't felt strong enough.

"The leg's better now," I said.

"Bullshit. You still limp."

"Not as much. And when I workout, I feel the strength again."

"But you still have metal pins in it."

"Lots of players play with pins."

"Have you told Rob yet?" she asked. Rob was her brother, the Chargers fourth wide receiver. Rob had introduced me to Cindy during college.

"Yes."

"What does he think?"

"He thinks it's a good idea."

We stopped walking and leaned over the heavy wooden rail. The air was suffused with brine and salt. Waves crashed beneath us, whitecaps glowing in the moonlight. A lifeguard Jeep was parked next to us, a quarter into the ocean on the pier. All that extra weight on the pier made me nervous.

"Why now?" she asked finally.

"My window is rapidly closing," I said.

"Not to mention you've always wondered if you could do it."

"Not to mention."

"And you're frustrated out of your gourd that a fucking leg injury has prevented you from finding this out."

"Such language from an anthropologist."

She sighed and hugged me around my waist. She was exactly a foot shorter than me, which made hugging easy, and kissing difficult.

"So what do you think?" I asked.

"I think you're frustrated and angry and that you need to do this."

"Not to mention I might just make a hell of a fullback."

"Is he the one who throws the ball?"

We had gone over this precisely one hundred and two times.

"No, but close."

She snuggled closer, burying her sharp chin deep into my side. It tickled. If I wasn't so tough I would have laughed.

"Just don't get yourself hurt."

"I don't plan to, but these things have a way of taking you by surprise."

"So are you really that good?" she asked, looking up at me.

"I'm going to find out."

She looked away. "If you make the team, things will change."

I hugged her tighter. "I know."

CHAPTER FOUR

I was in a conference room at the Orange County jail in Santa Ana, accompanied by Charley Brown's assistant, Mary Cho. We were alone, waiting for Derrick Booker to make his grand appearance. Mary was Chinese and petite and pretty. She wore a blue power suit, with the hem just above her knees. She sat next to me, and from our close proximity I had a clear view of her knees. Nice knees. Cho was probably still a law student. Probably worked out a whole lot. Seemed a little uptight, but nothing a little alcohol couldn't fix. Was probably a little tigress in bed. She wasn't much of a talker and seemed immune to my considerable charm. Probably because she had caught me looking at her knees.

The heavy door with the wire window opened and Derrick was shown into the conference room by two strapping wardens. He was left alone with us, the wardens waiting just outside the door. The kid himself was manacled and hogtied. Should he make a run for it, Pope John Paul II himself could have caught him from behind.

Mary Cho sprang to life, brightening considerably, leaning forward and gesturing to a chair opposite us.

"Derrick, thanks for meeting us," she said.

He shrugged, raising his cuffed hands slightly. "As if I had anything better to do."

Which is what I would have said. I stifled a grin. I suspected grins were illegal in the Orange County jail. Derrick sounded white, although he tried to hide that fact with a lot of swaggering showmanship. In fact, he sounded white *and* rich, with a slightly arrogant lilt to his voice. He was good looking, with strong features and light brown eyes. He was tall and built like an athlete.

"I have someone here who wants to speak with you," said Cho.

"Who? Whitey?"

I raised my hand. "That would be me."

Derrick's father owned lots of real estate across southern California, and Derrick himself had grown up filthy rich. He was about as far from the ghetto as you could get. Yet here he was, sounding as if he had lived the mean streets all his life. As if he had grown up in poverty, rather than experiencing the best Orange County had to offer, which is considerable. I suspected here in prison he was in survival mode, where being a wealthy black kid is as bad as being a wealthy white kid. Except that he had the jargon wrong and a few years out of date, and he still sounded upper class, no matter how hard he tried to hide it.

"My name's Jim Knighthorse."

"Hey, I know you, man!"

"Who doesn't?" I said. "And those who don't, should."

He smiled, showing a row of perfect white teeth. "How's your leg? Saw you bust it up against Miami. Hell, I wanted to throw up."

"I did throw up. You play?"

"Yeah. Running back."

"You any good?" I asked.

"School is full of whities, what do you think?"

I shrugged. "Some whities can run."

He grinned again. "Yeah, no shit. You could run, bro. Dad says wasn't for your leg you'd be in the pros."

"Still might."

"No shit?"

"No shit."

"What about the leg?" he asked.

"We'll see about the leg," I said.

We were silent. Derrick was losing the ghetto speak. His eyes had brightened considerably with the football talk. We looked at each other. Down to business.

"You do her, Derrick?"

"Do her?"

"He means kill her, Derrick," said Cho. "He's asking if you killed Amanda Peterson."

"Thank you, assistant Cho," I said, smiling at her. She looked away quickly. Clearly she didn't trust herself around me. I looked back at Derrick. "You kill her, Derrick?"

"Hell, no."

His arms flexed. Bulbous veins stood out against his forearms, disappearing up the short sleeves of his white prison attire. I could see those arms carrying a football.

"Why should anyone believe you?" I asked.

"Give a fuck what anyone believes."

"They found the knife in your car, Derrick. Her blood was on the knife. It adds up."

He was trying for hostile bad-ass, but he was just a kid, and eventually his emotions won out. They rippled across his expressive face, brief glimpses into his psyche: disbelief, rage, frustration. But most of all I saw *sorrow*. Deep sorrow.

"Because..." He stopped, swallowed, looked away. "Because we were going to get married."

"Married?"

"Uh huh."

"How old are you?"

"Seventeen."

"How old was she?"

"The same."

"Anyone know about the marriage?" I asked.

He laughed hollowly. "Hell, no. Her dad hates me, and I'm sure he doesn't think much of me now."

"I wouldn't imagine he does," I said. "You have any theories who might have killed her?"

He hesitated. "No."

"Was she seeing anyone else?"

"No."

"You were exclusive?"

"Yes."

"How do you know?"

"She loved me."

"Did you love her?" I asked.

He didn't answer immediately. The silence that followed was palpable. The ticking of the clock behind us accentuated the silence and gave it depth and profundity. I listened to him breathe through his mouth. The corners of his mouth were flecked with dried spittle.

"Yeah, I loved her," he said finally. He swiped his sleeve across his face, using a shrugging motion to compensate for his cuffed wrists. The sleeve was streaked with tears.

"That will be enough, Mr. Knighthorse," said Cho. "Thank you, Derrick."

She got up and went to the door. She knocked on the window and the two wardens entered and led the shuffling Derrick out of the room. He didn't look back. I got up and stood by the door with Cho.

"What do you think?" she asked.

"I think you're secretly in love with me," I said.

"I think you're secretly in love with yourself."

"It's no secret," I said.

We left the conference room and moved down the purposefully bare-walled hallway. Perhaps colorful paintings would have given the accused false hope.

"The kid didn't do her," I said. "No one's that good an actor."

She nodded. "We know. He's going to need your help."

"He's going to need a lot of help," I said.

"Let me guess: and you're the man to do it?"

"Took the words right out of my mouth."

ABOUT THE AUTHOR

J.R. Rain is an ex-private investigator who now writes full-time in the Pacific Northwest. He lives in a small house on a small island with his small dog, Sadie, who has more energy than Robin Williams.

Please visit him at www.jrrain.com.
Add him on Facebook.
Add him on Twitter.

CPSIA information can be obtained
at www.ICGtesting.com
Printed in the USA
LVHW092209230320
651002LV00002B/473